Spoiled Alicia

By
James Starvoice

© 2020 James Starvoice
All rights reserved. No part of this book may be reproduced or transmitted in any form or by any means, electronic, mechanical, photocopying, recording, or otherwise, without prior written permission of the author.
ISBN-13: 9798679390911

CONTENTS

Title 001

Contents 003

Acknowledgment 005

Chapter 01: Rumor Has It 007

Chapter 02: Alicia's Decision 016

Chapter 03: Alicia & Chicken 029

Chapter 04: Alicia & Egg 044

Chapter 05: Alicia & Playmate 055

Chapter 06: Alicia & Bodyguard 076

Chapter 07: Alicia & Peephole 089

Chapter 08: Alicia & the Devil 100

Chapter 09: Alicia & Priest 111

Chapter 10: Alicia & Permanent Solution 121

Chapter 11: Alicia & the Blacksmith Who Saved the Day 135

Chapter 12: Alicia & New Design 144

Chapter 13: Alicia & New Order 153

Thank You! 166

ACKNOWLEDGMENT

My gratitude to,

Stephanie Hoogstad

whom despite battling with fire ant invasion
in her kitchen was able to edit this book to the best
it can ever be.

Thank you,

James Starvoice

Chapter 1

Rumor Has It...

Gentle dew on green leaves glistened brilliantly as the first light of dawn shined on the small Bavarian town of Füssen.

Olga, a newly wed bride, rose from her hay-stuffed mattress at the break of dawn to the crowing of roosters. Careful not to wake the man sleeping next to her, she seated herself on the mattress and took her time dressing in her dirndl—a customary dress consisting of a bodice, skirt, blouse, and apron.

After she secured the lacing and tied her long blond hair up in a ribbon, she smiled tenderly to the face of her beloved, Diedrich.

Her man may have owned nothing, was a little stubborn and whiny, and behaved stupidly sometimes, but she loved him more than life itself, and she couldn't feel prouder of him for how hard he'd been working to support their small nest over the past months.

She will not feel the warmth of his arms again until dusk when he return from the farm, and he will probably be bone-tired again. Such is spring to a farmer: a rush of work to get crops in the ground before the weeds take over.

There was nothing Olga could do about that. What she *could* do was let the love of her life sleep a little longer. She fixed the sheets to better protect him from cold, left a dish of cheese and bread on the table for when he wakes up, grabbed her butter-separator, and headed out to tend her father's cows.

Shutting the door of their cottage behind her, she blinked rapidly from the blinding sunlight, and smiled. For Olga, this was to be just another peaceful spring day at Füssen.

Little did Olga know that over the next two days she was going to do something that would turn their quiet town on its head.

* * *

"Olga, good morning!"

"Good morning, Mr. Kunibert." Olga stopped to greet her caller, balancing a basket full of bricks of butter against her hip.

The old man, Mr. Kunibert, looked like the devil. His skin wrinkled, his eyes a glowing yellow, slick, gray hair hung to his shoulders. His hands and apron were wet with blood from the chickens he butchered at the table of his shop that was strategically located at the head of the market.

Olga never let his looks bother her. She knew Mr. Kunibert was a very nice person, albeit a little on the perverted side.

"Is that today's butter?" he asked.

"I've just churned and salted it."

"I'll take one."

"Of course." She approached the table and held out a brick of butter for him. "Freshly made by my own hands.

Mr. Kunibert turned to wash his hands. He then took the brick but withdrew his other hand—the one holding the payment—before Olga could take the coin.

He jested, eyes on her magnificent bosom, "Wooh! Didn't you strap your laces a bit too tightly this morning?"

"Mr. Kunibert." Olga rolled her eyes, her hand still in the air.

"How can you breathe like that? Loosen it up a little. I can help you, if you like."

She raised her voice, almost yelping. "Mr. Kunibert!" Smiling wildly, she signaled *'give me, give me'* with her extended hand. "My Pfenninc," she reminded him, "or do you mean to eat my butter for free?"

Mr. Kunibert comically looked left and right before leaning his upper half over the table to whisper, "Free or not, I'll eat *your butter* any day."

She hopped on her toes and threw her head back in hopelessness.

"What? I was talking about *this butter*." He chuckled, playing with the brick in his hand. "What else did you think I meant?"

"Give me that!"

Laughing, Mr. Kunibert withdrew his hand before she could take the butter from him. He handed her the coin.

Olga said with a pretended sigh, "Thank you." She then decided to tease the old man back. Smiling, she held the coin in front of her face between her index and middle finger. "I'd have you know, I've got nothing against dirty old men, so long as they pay first, joke later." She tucked the coin in her cleavage.

Mr. Kunibert cracked a laugh. "You vixen! No wonder that basket always returns empty. I swear, Diedrich is the luckiest dog ever."

"I know he is. No woman alive can fill my shoes," she replied haughtily.

Mr. Kunibert snapped as if her words made him recall something. He bent forward and signaled for Olga to lean closer. "Oh, this reminds me, come here, there's a secret I must tell you."

Olga narrowed her gaze. "You just want to look down my bodice again."

"No, I'm serious, you've got to hear this."

She leaned toward him and whispered, "What?"

"Listen, oh, praise the Lord, you will not believe this. You must promise not to tell anyone."

"What? Tell me."

"You know that our lord Ludwig has left to Dusseldorf, right?"

"Everyone knows. We bid him farewell yesterday. So what?"

"Sooo, I've heard from a very reliable source…*Spoiled Alicia*. She's planning on coming to town today."

Olga set her palm to the side of his head and gave him a push just as she retreated. She scorned dismissively, "What a load of nonsense."

Spoiled Alicia

"I'm serious."

"I'm sure she will."

"You don't believe me? Then wait and see for yourself. Spoiled Alicia—"

"Don't call her *spoiled*. These are but her ungrateful maids telling false gossips behind her back. If the guards hear you, you could lose your tongue. And one more thing: she will come down here and *do what,* hm? Have you thought about that?"

"Perhaps…perhaps she wants to—"

"Buy one of your chickens, maybe?"

Irritated, Mr. Kunibert pulled a chicken by its legs out of a cage and showed it to Olga. "Maybe she will! As a matter of fact, I'm already prepared. I'm saving my fattest chicken for when she walks by and will give it to her as a gift."

It sounded so stupid, Olga glared at him with a narrow gaze, "You can't be serious."

"You know nothing about how this world works. Her father is *the lord*. If…if…if by some chance it really happened and I can gift her something that will make her happy, it will reach her father's ears. Do you even know what that means?"

Smiling with silliness and nodding her head, she

joked, "Her father will buy a chicken from you every morning. Maybe two."

"Very funny. Laugh all you like now, but when I drown in riches, guess who will be the first at my door, asking for a loan?"

Olga waved her hand in the air. "Yes, yes, yes, I'll learn from your example and save my *softest brick of butter* for when I see her, so that I, too, will drown in riches." She snapped with pretended shock. "Oh, no, wait, I totally forgot. I must first beg your wise guidance. Please tell me: what…does…Alicia…*look like*?"

Met by silence, Olga walked away, laughing over her shoulder. "I thought so."

Mr. Kunibert yelled after her, "Laugh. Yes, laugh while you still can. I swear, I should not have told you. You'll see, I'll figure it out."

Ignoring him, Olga waved at a woman walking in the opposite direction. "Good morning, Mrs. Muller."

"Good morning, my dear."

Olga stopped on her way, giggling and covering her mouth as she recalled the irritated look on Mr. Kunibert's face and his absurd secret.

She sent her gaze south, beyond the log-built town's

church and green woods at its background, towards the great castle atop the hill overlooking their town.

Here, within the town's market, was the closest Olga or any of her friends had ever been to the castle.

It looked so grand and so beautiful with its white walls and towers. She wondered to herself in which of those beautiful towers Alicia lived. Was she truly the apple of her father's eye, as it was told? What was her daily life like? And what was she doing right now?

For but a moment, Olga allowed doubt to whisper in her ear: *What if* the news Mr. Kunibert told her was real? *What if* Spoiled Alicia truly intended to come down to town? And *why…?*

It was rumored that Alicia was descended from a line of twenty-one princesses.

It was rumored that Alicia had never taken a step outside her room and rose gardens before.

It was rumored that, once, Alicia wanted to attend a mass, so her father built her her own church within the castle walls, and when Alicia didn't find her picture among the triptych of Jesus, the Virgin Mary, and saints, it was said that she cried until the tears drenched her dress and ordered the church demolished.

It was rumored that the carpets of her room were

replaced daily. That her bath was made of marble. Her bed of clouds. Her hairbrush of gold. That her maids outnumbered her father's army, and her pets were even more numerous.

And it was rumored that… Alicia wasn't even real.

Olga shook her head and laughed at herself for even considering such falsehoods. It was surely nonsense. No such a person could possibly exist.

Spoiled Alicia, if not a fairytale, was but an innocent child fallen victim to her own maids' jealousy.

Leave the fairytales for the fools.

For now, Olga had fresh butter to sell.

Spoiled Alicia

Chapter 2

Alicia's Decision

While Olga, the town of Füssen, and the whole world woke up to the crowing of roosters, this was who awoke Alicia up every morning...

No one!

Once, in her younger years, the crowing of a rooster disturbed Alicia's sleep. It upset her. The damn rooster just wouldn't shut up. Alicia complained to her father who, thus, decreed every rooster be killed within five hundred paces from the castle walls and every crow and noisy bird shot down on sight.

Not a single rooster had been heard in the castle ever since.

In her room, high in the tower, with her beautiful blond hair spread under her head, twelve-year-old Alicia slept soundly on her huge bed, covered with pure-white silk sheets embraided with the first letter of her name in golden threads, and surrounded by her maids-in-waiting.

The only persons moving a limb between the four

white walls decorated with paintings and golden frames were her two fanning-maids, who monitored their mistress's face carefully for any sign of discomfort as they fanned Alicia with just the right amount of breeze. Another was near a stand, gently fanning incense smoke across the room.

As Alicia turned and moaned in her sleep, her bird-maid followed, hurrying from one side of bed to the other—wherever her mistress turned her face—whilst holding a golden cage in her hands with two finches inside, for that Alicia believed it brought her good luck to see finches first thing in the morning.

Alicia moaned as she opened her deep blue eyes. "Birdy... Good morning." She sleepily reached out her hand near the cage and rubbed her fingers as if to feed them.

The bird-maid sprinkled seeds from atop the cage, alongside Alicia's motion.

Young Alicia then looked at the foot of her bed and saw the fifty-year-old head-maid, Madam Schneider, signaling the female performers with her hand to start playing soft music before she, and every woman in the room, curtsied in unison.

As the music played, two of her dressing-maids helped Alicia to her feet while four others stepped forth and held sheets in between themselves to conceal the trio, their backs to their mistress as the two maids undressed Alicia.

Nothing fancy. These were but the morning crew. It was said that Alicia had one hundred forty dressing-maids alone and could decide on a whim to change her outfit as many as seven times a day.

Her dress was passed on the hands of one maid to the next until it was received by the dressing-maids behind the sheets. Madam Schneider monitored the process with much attention.

"No," Alicia said.

Madam Schneider signaled the performers to stop playing.

"I don't like it. I want a rose dress."

"Of course," Madam Schneider said with a bow of her head.

Madam Schneider motioned the performers to continue playing as the dress Alicia rejected was handed back down the line and a rose-colored dress was sent the other way.

"Madam Schneider," Alicia called.

The maids stopped passing the dress, and Madam Schneider, again, silenced the performers. "Yes, Lady Alicia?"

"I've changed my mind. I'll have my bath before breakfast."

"As you wish."

Before Madam Schneider could issue the new instructions, Alicia said again, "It's not too cold today, is it?"

"No, my lady. In fact, it's very lovely."

"Then I'll have it at the balcony."

"Of course."

Madam Schneider signaled the performers to play. The rose dress was sent back from where it came from and a cream shirt was sent forth instead. Meanwhile, Madam Schneider opened the door and sent a maid hurrying down the stairs to carry out her lady's wishes.

Four burly slaves entered the room carrying a stretcher with a tub strapped to it. Following them was a line of servants carrying buckets of hot water. Once the tub was set on the balcony and filled with water and rose petals and the male slaves retreated, Alicia's dressing-maids removed the sheets concealing her.

Dressed in the thin cream shirt, Alicia headed to the balcony where her bathing-maids awaited and Madam Schneider was adding drips of perfume to the tub, after having checked the temperature.

Spoiled Alicia

Alicia entered the tub, in her shirt, with the help of her bathing-maids. She relaxed the back of her head on the provided cushion, closed her eyes, and sighed as her bathing-maids worked on her.

* * *

Mr. Weber, a councilor of the castle, was a bellied man in his fifties with a short, pointy, black beard and small eyebrows. He stood across the dining table in his feathered Tudor bonnet, tight black pants, brown furry overcoat with fluffy shoulders and glittering copper buttons.

Alongside Mr. Weber was another councilor: Mr. Meyer. He dressed similarly to his companion but was at least a decade younger and much slimmer, always had his hands joined at his chest, and didn't like wearing hats. His thick bowl-like brown hair made him look more like a monk.

Mr. Weber continued reading a report with the provincialism and clear voice of a prominent castle appointee, "The second messenger we received this morning brought word that our lord, your father, has departed safely from the town of Prasberg on his way to meet the nobles at Dusseldorf. We are all, of course, praying for his safe return and keeping a close eye on his news. May my lady's heart rest at ease—"

As Mr. Weber spoke and soft music played in the grand dining hall with great crystal chandeliers, painted ceiling, decorated walls, and marble floors, Alicia sat fifty feet away at the magnificent table having her breakfast.

Her maids lined the wall behind her. Armored castle guards were stationed at the entrances. Next to Alicia, a high stand was set, engraved similarly to her own seat, with one of her pets—a small dog dressed in a collar with diamonds—eating cream inlaid with diced fruit from a plate of gold.

This was what Alicia had on her plate…

She didn't have one!

Plates were for dogs. For pets. For commoners.

For Alicia, a breakfast-maid would approach with a covered silver dish at hand, curtsy, and reveal the dish.

Should Alicia blink twice—for she believed it was improper to speak during a meal—the dish was rejected, the breakfast-maid would move on, and another will bring in the next dish. If Alicia approved it with an elegant nod of her head, the breakfast-maid would approach the table. Another breakfast-maid stationed to Alicia's right side would receive a silver spoon enwrapped with a white kerchief from the one standing next to her, scoop, and feed Alicia.

Spoiled Alicia

The breakfast-maid to Alicia's left would then take a folded kerchief from a tray—held by the one standing next to her—and wipe Alicia's lips with it.

One spoonful, and the dish made space for the next one—spoon and kerchief replaced.

"Which brings us to the most important matter at hand for today…" Mr. Weber said as he reached the end of his report. He took two pieces of fabric from a servant and exhibited them to Alicia with a big smile. "Which color does our lady like best for her new curtains, hm? Personally, I recommend the green-and-gold. It truly catches the essence of the season, wouldn't you say?"

Alicia raised her hand, interrupting the breakfast process.

The breakfast-maid to her left attempted to wipe her lady's lips, but Alicia, who looked suddenly upset, snatched the kerchief from her hand. "I can do it myself."

Seeing this, Madam Schneider signaled the rest of the maids, who retreated from Alicia's table, and the music stopped playing.

Alicia took her time wiping her lips properly before she looked at the councilor. "Mr. Weber. Why are you bothering me with this?"

He said, "I sincerely apologize if the timing wasn't

to your pleasure."

"No," she said. "I meant, why *this* issue in particular?" She glared at him for a short pause. "The color of my curtains? News of my father who departed less than a day ago? A sick pet? What are you trying to do?"

"I-I thought it was your wish, my lady, to be informed of every important little detail. You insist on it, in fact. As for the curtains, I've taken great lengths to determine which will suit—"

"Mr. Weber," she interrupted, "allow me to rephrase: what, exactly, are you trying to distract me from?"

Mr. Weber froze. His scheme didn't miss her vigilance. He handed the fabric back to his servant and faced Alicia with it, bluntly, "Princess Alicia. I received word that my lady intends to go to the town, today."

"I do."

"I must urge you not to. It's, um, for your own safety."

"My safety?" Alicia raised an eyebrow. "From an enemy?"

"Not—no, no!"

"We have a war going on at Füssen?"

Mr. Weber was cornered. "No-um-ut," he turned to

his colleague for help, "Mr. Meyer!"

"Of course not," Mr. Meyer said. "Lady Alicia, I believe what Mr. Weber is trying to say is that *the town* is simply no place for a young lady such as yourself."

"Yes. That's exactly right. It's improper, to say the least," said Mr. Weber.

Alicia stared at him for a little pause, then at Mr. Meyer and Madam Schneider. She said to her pets-maid, "Wipe Pochy's mouth and take him for a walk."

"Yes, my lady."

Alicia then abandoned her seat. "Mr. Weber." She approached him.

Mr. Weber stiffened and exchanged looks with Madam Schneider, who was clearly just as concerned.

"Remind me," Alicia said, "who is the head of this castle in absence of my father?"

"You, of course, my lady."

"And his duty to my people. Is it not mine, now?" She stood in front of him.

"Well, that depends. I mean, under the circumstances, considering your young age and…" He swallowed. "I mean, yes."

She continued to stare up at him, so he leaned down and said softly, "But that doesn't mean there's any need for you to go down *theeere*. Lady Alicia, it's a long way. The stairs. The castle bridge. The weather that can change at any moment. Why go through all of that? We have everything under control for you. Rest assured, everything is fine."

"Good," she spat, "and I want to see for myself that it is."

"*Aliciaaa*, please—"

She silenced him with a signal of her index finger. "You think I'm too young for this, don't you?"

His face sweaty, he wiped his forehead with a kerchief. "That's not really the problem."

She replied with a determination of steel, "I'd have you know, Mr. Weber, that I've had the best mentors and education this world has to offer. I've read more books about history alone than all who can read in Füssen could finish in a lifetime. And in every one of those books, the first thing a good king does is go, in disguise, among his people to see how they're doing. Well, I am the dominar of my people now, and I've made up my mind on my first move."

"Well, um, did these good kings really have to? I mean—" Alicia walked away. He called after her, "Couldn't they just see how the people were doing from the balcony? The wind is, is, quite refreshing and—"

"Don't worry, Mr. Weber. Mr. Lang will accompany me," Alicia said as she walked, signaling at Mr. Lang—the commander of the castle guard.

"But, but—"

She offered her hand to one of her nails-maids. "And I will be *in disguise*. So, why the unnecessary worry? I just want to see how the people are doing, that's all." She continued as her nails were painted, "No one will even notice I was there. In fact, I'll be taking nothing with me but what is deemed essential."

Alicia looked at her nails-maid. The maid looked back at her.

"You're essential," Alicia said, causing Madam Schneider to rub the side of her temple and Mr. Weber to sigh with worry.

* * *

This was how Alicia went in disguise…

The royal coach was the size of a small room. A red carpet covered the middle section of the wooden floor. The oil lamps were made of gold. The benches had fluffy wine cushions—same as the curtains—with a golden string running along their edges. In the middle of the coach stood a table that could be lowered, and the benches flipped and fixed over it to form a bed occupying the entire coach's space so that Alicia could sleep in comfort if she wished.

Alicia wore a white dress embraided with a floral pattern, not to attract attention to herself. Furthermore—having learned from her books and mentors that commoners were, overwhelmingly, poor—she wore a single oval ruby, the size of her thumb, to make sure she blended in with the local women.

Following her was a small army of fifty mounted knights and twice as many maids. This was the first time Alicia's travel-maids were ever called to serve, so the three women with her and the two more standing on the rear steps of the coach were quiet nervous.

Reaching the town's gate, the coach stopped. Mr. Lang knocked on the door. "Princess Alicia. We've arrived."

Anxious yet eager for adventure, Alicia couldn't restrain her smile as she watched her maids open the door and a short red carpet rolled onto the town's street.

"This is it," she whispered to herself and stepped down.

A large crowd of excited villagers had already surrounded the coach. When they saw Alicia step down, they had little doubt in their minds who that was. They cheered, called her name, and tried to push past the guards, who had formed a circle to keep the crowd under control.

Stunned speechless, Alicia turned her face among the faces of crowd, then looked back at her coach and said quietly to herself, "Curses. The coach gave me away."

To her own admiration, Alicia handled the unexpected situation quite well. She summoned a smile of royalty and stepped forth, waving her hand to the crowd. She heard a man's voice so loud, it towered above the hype.

"Princess Alicia, Princess Alicia!"

Confused, Alicia turned towards the voice and saw Mr. Kunibert at his shop, holding a chicken in the air by its legs. Before she could comprehend what he intended to do, Mr. Kunibert shouted, "This is for you!"

He slapped the chicken across the table and chopped off its head with a single clean swing.

The sight of blood.

Alicia's eyes widened with horror.

She fainted.

Chapter 3

Alicia & Chicken

Dressed in a white sleeping shirt, Alicia lay on her bed surrounded by quietness and dim lights. The voices of her nursing-maids and doctors could vaguely be heard from across the door.

Suddenly, Alicia sprang up from her sleep, yelling as mad as a woman in a nightmare, "GUARDS! MAIDS! EVERYBODY!"

The doors flew opened, her maids and doctors surrounded the bed, and a great hype rattled the place as everyone spoke at once, inquiring how Alicia was doing.

Their voices soon went down as every eye in the room fixed on Alicia, waiting for her to speak.

Her eyes down, her face maimed by a hard expression, and her little fists clinched to the sheets, she hissed, "Summon my War Council."

Shocked silent, no one knew what to say.

Spoiled Alicia

A nursing-maid faked a smile. "Princess Alicia, the most important thing right now is: how do you feel? Are you hurt? Does it hurt, anywhere? The doctors worry you might have—"

She shouted, "No doctors. This is more important!"

"Yes, of course, but—"

Another maid spoke from the opposite end, gaining Alicia's face, "My lady, we'll send word immediately, of course. But the doctors must check on you and, um, if you say that you wish to send them away, that's fine. But it's almost lunch time. The least you must do is eat something first. It's your duty to yourself. You must not take your health lightly."

Alicia thought it over for a moment. "Fine."

Her maids sighed with relief.

She pushed the sheets off herself and slid off the bed. "Summon them to the dining hall. This can't wait."

* * *

Alicia's lunch-maids stood to one side of the dining hall, holding dishes at hand, whereas Madam Schneider, Mr. Weber, Mr. Meyer, and Mr. Lang, flocked by the captains of the castle guards, waited at the center of the hall for Alicia's arrival, exchanging blame among themselves.

Madam Schneider hissed, "This is all your fault. I warned you about this with ample time. You should have done something."

Mr. Weber responded quietly, "I did all that I could do to dissuade her."

"She didn't last three steps. When the lord hears about this, he will have our heads."

"I said I did all that I could do," he turned to Mr. Meyer, waving his finger in the air, "whereas YOU should have done a better job backing me up. You barely spoke three words atop each other. What in heaven's name was that?"

"Was it really as bad as your attempt to distract her with the *color* of her new curtains?" Mr. Meyer mocked.

"Well, I didn't exactly see you try."

"If there's anyone to blame in this hall, it would be Mr. Lang."

Mr. Lang came in front of Mr. Meyer. "Say what? My men did their job perfectly. No one lay a finger on her."

"SHE is only twelve," Mr. Weber countered. "What's more, she's not used to such hectic situations. Of course the crowd freaked her out."

"Then why did you let her out in the first place? You

created this mess."

"It was your responsibility. You should have done a better job controlling the crowd."

A maid, hurrying on her toes, entered the hall to announce, "Princess Alicia is on her way."

Mr. Weber dismissed her, "Yes, thank you."

They stood, quiet and at attention...

Madam Schneider leaned sideways at Mr. Weber to whisper, "Did you really summon the bannermen to a war council?"

He glared at her. "Are you implying that *I* could have possibly disregarded a direct order from my monarch?" He faced forward, stiff and silent, then whispered, "Mr. Meyer?"

"I told the messengers to be on standby, just in case, so we will not have to call them back later."

"Excellent."

Alicia, dressed in red and black, entered the dining hall with fire in her eyes. A maid pulled a seat for her, but Alicia was so mad, she signaled the maid to hold and glared at her council instead.

After a pause full of tension, she hissed, "Everything is under control... Everything is just *fiiine*... That's what you assured me this morning, wasn't it?" She assumed her seat. "First time I go down to Füssen, and *there*, right under my nose, I WITNESS A CRIME!"

"*A crime...?*" Mr. Weber echoed as he, and the rest stared daggers at a clueless Mr. Lang. He turned back to Alicia. "A crime, you say, my lady?"

"A CRIME!" She shouted, "I want the army to deal with this AT ONCE."

"Of course, my lady. No crime must go unpunished. Rest assured that your council will never tolerate such a thing," said Mr. Weber. "However, if I may inquire, what kind of a crime did you say you witnessed?"

Madam Schneider glared at him. "Are you questioning our lady's word, *her own testimony*?"

He raised his voice with impatience. "I AM SAYING: depending on the nature of the crime, there might be other, less severe methods to handle it than summoning the lord's entire army and bannermen, as I'm sure Lady Alicia will agree."

"A murder," Alicia said, her eyes watery suddenly. "Severe enough for you?"

"A murder...?" Mr. Weber, and the rest, slowly turned to glare at Mr. Lang. "A MURDER?"

Mr. Meyer raged, "What were your men doing?"

Mr. Lang stammered, "I-I didn't see, I mean, no! No

such thing. I was there. The princess is mistaken, she fell and hurt her head."

"HURT HER HEAD?" Mr. Weber yelled.

Madam Schneider gasped. She snapped at him, "You said your men caught her in time. You said she never touched the ground."

"I didn't, really, see what was—"

"Outrageous incompetence!" Mr. Weber said with disgust. He then raised his voice, silencing Mr. Lang before he could speak again, "I THINK I'VE HEARD ENOUGH! No more excuses from you. I will handle this now."

Mr. Weber turned to Alicia. "Princess Alicia, if you'd be so kind, tell me what exactly happened down there?"

Sniffling, she said, "There was a man, a horrible, horrible man, kin to the devil himself. He-he, as soon as I stepped down the coach, he had this huge knife, it was like he wanted me to see it, and he, he," she covered her mouth, fighting back tears, "he killed it."

"Killed it?"

"*Yesss*," she squeaked, on the verge of tears.

Confused, he asked again, "Killed, what? I mean, who?"

"An innocent creature. A *biiird*… The monster."

Mr. Weber froze. He waited for Alicia to pull herself together. "A bird, my lady…? Big white bird? An old man with long, gray hair? His shop is at the beginning of the market?"

"Yes," Alicia said after a sniffle, using all her strength to assume the strong stance a royalty should uphold before her subject. "Yes. That's the one. Now, I know what you think, that I might be overreacting. That the taking of the life of a bird is not the same as people. But you were not there, Mr. Weber. You did not witness the horrors I saw." She motioned with her head. "Take command of as many men you need. I want this hideous crime dealt with, immediately."

Surrounded by awkward silence, Mr. Weber looked left and right, but no one stepped forth to aid him. Even Madam Schneider—who suddenly realized that Alicia had never seen a living chicken in her life—looked away, covering her face with her palm.

Mr. Lang whispered mockingly, "You said you want to handle it."

Mr. Weber whispered back, "*Shut up.*"

Mr. Weber then cleared his voice and turned to Alicia. He addressed her formally, strongly, with no indication of sarcasm whatsoever.

"Lady Alicia, we understand your concerns and your feelings. The kindness of your heart is *truly*... remarkable.

NOBLE! Yes. So noble, indeed, it puts our souls to shame. However, I must ask you to understand that it was, it was only a chicken."

Alicia jumped to her feet, raging, "Mr. Weber, are you taking me for a fool?"

"Princess—"

"A chicken? Mr. Weber, if you are trying to comfort me, then you could not have picked a worse time for a joke. I know what I saw. That was no chicken. It was a living, innocent, feathery, charming creature, and that man MURDERED IT."

Madam Schneider set her palm on Mr. Weber's shoulder and took initiative. "Lady Alicia. If I may say so, that was indeed a chicken."

Alicia snapped with disbelief, "Madam Schneider?"

"The man you saw was only doing his work, providing chicken to feed people."

Slapping her palm to the table, Alicia raged, "IT WAS NO CHICKEN."

"Did it sound like…" Madam Schneider started, but she hesitated. She looked around the room, surrounded by silence and anxiety, and whispered to a maid nearby, "You."

Nervous, the maid pointed at herself.

"Yes, you. Come here," Madam Schneider whispered.

When the maid came near, Madam Schneider set her palm on the maid's shoulder, turned her towards Alicia, and said, "Did it sound something like this?"

With an awkward look on her face, the maid looked over her shoulder at Madam Schneider—who motioned her to make the noise—then back to Alicia.

The maid said, "puk-puk... Puk-puk-puk-puk... puk?"

"No. NO!" Alicia snapped, "No, that is nothing like what it sounded like."

Madam Schneider whispered something in the maid's ear; it made the maid look back at her with widened eyes.

"*Please*," Madam Schneider begged.

The maid shut her eyes and inhaled deeply, bracing herself.

"PKAAAK! PUK-PUK-PUK! PAAAK! PAAAK! PAAAAK!"

Feeling shaken, Alicia muttered under her breath, "Yes."

"That, Lady Alicia, was a chicken," Madam Schneider said, patting the maid's shoulder—who returned to her spot covering her face with shame. "It's what a chicken looks and sounds like before it's cleaned and cooked."

Shocked to the core, Alicia sank into her seat,

muttering, "A... A chicken? That's what it..." She slowly turned her gaze from one face in the room to the next. "That's how...?"

"Yes."

"Ducks, too...? Pigeons...? *Geese?*"

Madam Schneider nodded. "The same."

Her lips trembled, "Swans...?"

Alicia turned her face to her lunch-maids.

The maids became restless on their feet, stealing looks at one of them and slowly distancing themselves from her. The maid they had pointed out looked so shaken she could barely stand. She set her hand on the dish she was holding, shut her eyes, and removed the cover—revealing the roasted swan.

Horrified, Alicia gasped and jumped to her feet, hands covering her mouth. She ran out of the hall.

Madam Schneider shut her eyes and rubbed her forehead.

"This is getting ridiculous," whispered Mr. Meyer.

Madam Schneider said under her breath, "Just don't tell her where red meat comes from, or the last time any of us will have any will be *yesterday's dinner.*"

* * *

Alicia ran into the corridor leading to the dining hall, where three of her maids clung to the walls, out of her way.

She stopped and called out, her voice a tone of misery, "Comfort... *Comfort.*"

None of the maids moved; they just stared worriedly at one another.

Alicia stomped her foot and blurted with despair, tears glistening on her cheeks, "Where is a comfort-maid when you need one!"

Spotting a kerchief in the hands of one of her maids—standing farther away from the other two—Alicia approached the maid. "You," she asked very quietly, "is that a tears kerchief?"

The maid responded with the same secrecy, "It's-it's a kerchief, my lady. A normal one."

With a whining tone, Alicia spun around herself, looking everywhere. She had no choice. "Is it clean?"

"Of course."

Alicia looked at the other two maids. "Go. Leave us!"

Once the two women exited the corridor, Alicia turned to the maid and held herself still, her chin high. "Quickly."

The maid carefully wiped off Alicia's tears for her.

"Quickly, before someone might see this."

"Just a moment more."

"Hurry."

"Almost done."

"If someone walks in on us, fold that kerchief in your palm before they might see it."

"I will… There. Done."

"Are you sure?"

"Yes. Not a trace."

Alicia suddenly grabbed the maid's hand, the one holding the kerchief, and hissed, "Destroy this kerchief. No one must ever hear of this, understand?"

"Yes, my lady, of course. Your secret dies with me."

Craving emotional contact, Alicia embraced the maid for a few moments. She then held the maid by her upper arms and looked her in the eye. "You are promoted to a comfort-maid."

The maid stammered, "I, it's an honor."

"You did well," Alicia assured her, patting the maid's upper arms. She took a step back. "How do I look?"

The maid reached out her hand, hesitated for a moment, then went for it and fixed a lock of hair back over Alicia's ear. "Perfect. The stars shy with jealousy."

"Excellent." Alicia spun on her heel towards the dining

hall's entrance and inhaled a deep breath. "Now, stay close. You might be needed."

"Yes."

She marched back towards the hall, comfort-maid at her wing.

* * *

Entering the dining hall with the elegance of a woman and the aura of a leader, Alicia silenced the whispers and made her council stiffened.

Assuming her seat, Alicia asked, "What else do I need to know about these—*practices*? *Hmm*? Any other living creatures deformed into meals by that man? Sausages? Cheese? *Steak*, perhaps?"

"No, no, no," they all replied in unison and shook their heads.

"Of course, not. Not by him, I'm quite sure."

"None that comes to mind at the moment."

Alicia asked again, "I'm not going to find out later that he throws living bulls on his table and chop their heads off for meat, am I?"

"That would be physically impossible for him," said Mr.

Spoiled Alicia

Meyer.

Mr. Lang whispered to Madam Schneider, "*She's never seen a bull before?*"

"*In her books, all animal pictures are drawn of the same size.*"

"*Ah!*"

"It's a, a completely different process, in my opinion." Mr. Weber promised, "It's nothing like the chicken, I assure you. There aren't even, hah, any feathers to strip! No. No. These are two completely different lines of business conducted by different professions. No need to bother yourself with the details, of course, as it can be quite boring."

"Good." Alicia inhaled deeply then declared, "All things considered. I cannot allow this to continue any longer."

Silence…

Her council looked at one another. Mr. Weber asked, "Allow what to continue, my lady?"

"This SAVAGERY!" She slammed her palm to the table, causing them to hop to their toes with shock. "It's a horrible practice. Barbaric. Unchristian. It is hideous. Hideous and criminal and disgusting. The Lord, Jesus, will not allow it. *I* will not allow it." She paused to calm her rage then resumed, "As of today, I forbid the killing and…" she shut her eyes with horribleness, "and *eating*, of chickens, ducks, pigeons, geese, and especially swans. This evil ends here."

Madam Schneider whispered, "I saw this coming."

Mr. Meyer whispered back, "I say we keep the damage to minimum until the lord returns." He saw Mr. Weber and Mr. Lang secretly nod with approval, so he cleared his voice and took a step forward, "If that is our lady's wish, this council approves and will carry out your decree. As of this moment: it is forbidden to slaughter all of the creatures you've mentioned within the castle walls. And I will see to it myself that the cooks understand this thoroughly."

Alicia stared daggers at him.

Mr. Meyer swallowed. He faked a chuckle. "Certainly, um, certainly my lady doesn't mean in Füssen, too… Do you?"

Alicia jumped to her feet and, in her rage, slammed her palms to the table, shouting, "AND IN ALL THE LAND UNDER MY DOMAIN!"

Chapter 4

Alicia & Egg

This was how Alicia read her books…

Late that night, Alicia sat at her grand desk in the castle library, her maids ever by her side. One reading-maid held Alicia's cup of posset—hot milk curdled with wine—watering Alicia's lips with small sips, on spoons of silver.

She was upset and not really into reading, just signaling a reading-maid with her finger to flip the pages of the book placed on a vertical stand on the desk, back and forth.

The room featured grand paintings surrounded by golden frames over pure white walls, fancy chairs with fluffy wine-cushions, and engraved tables with golden edges, burdened with vases of roses.

The books lined the shelves above and can only be reached by a spiral staircase made of two separate helixes with no central support, twisted together in a double helix formation. The staircase, painted the color of jade, branched overhead in four directions to the upper shelves.

Alicia huffed and signaled the maid to close the book.

"I can't read."

Her librarian, Mrs. Wagner, a woman in her thirties with long, curly black hair, approached Alicia, intending to comfort her. "Is my lady still upset?"

"After what I've seen today?" She huffed some more and tapped her fingers to the desk, thinking seriously. "I need to write my father about this."

A reading-maid brought paper and a quill pen with gold-tip, ready to script the letter. Alicia scolded her, "I haven't decided yet."

The maid took the tools away.

Mrs. Wagner said softly, "Lady *Aliciaaa*, please don't be upset, it was only a bad experience. It will come to pass. Personally, I think you handled things quite well today."

"You think?"

"Why, of course. I myself always had a soft spot for the poor creatures. It's horrible the way things are done. The human hypocrisy towards other beings' suffering, pain, and misery. It's terrible. In light of so many other food alternatives, I would say: it's even shameful."

Alicia snapped, "Exactly. Mrs. Wagner, that's exactly how I feel. How could no one else see it all this time?"

"I think you did a wonderful thing. Trust that the Lord

Spoiled Alicia

will not overlook the good you've done—it's as pure as the driven snow. Not only did you save so many poor creatures from suffering but, also, people will now have more eggs on their tables. I'm sure that, with time, it will dawn on them how kind and fruitful your decision is. There is nothing better than a long-run rewarding solution."

Alicia stared at her blankly.

"Something wrong?"

Confused, Alicia asked, "What do eggs got to do with chickens?"

Stunned, Mrs. Wagner froze for a moment. She faked a smile. "Oh, Alicia, you're so funny. Chickens lay eggs, of course."

"I know that," Alicia said. "Chickens are birds. Birds lay eggs. I know all of that. My question was: what does the quantity of eggs got to do with more chickens?"

Not sure she understood Alicia's point, Mrs. Wagner answered anyway, "Why, because chickens make them. So, naturally, the more chicken one has, the more eggs one will get."

"They make them? How?"

"How? Well, um, they just do."

"All right, so they make them, and then they lay them for us?"

"Yes, of course."

"With what?"

Startled, it suddenly dawned on Mrs. Wagner what the issue was. She tried to retreat. "Princess Alicia, tell you what, it's getting late. Perhaps you should get some sleep now, and we can talk about this in more detail later."

"What's there to talk about? It's a simple question." Alicia grabbed a Fabergé egg—egg made of diamonds and rubies—from her desk. "This is an egg. I'm now laying it *dooown* on my desk. See? I can do that because I've got hands. But birds don't have hands, so how do they do it? It's much too big to carry in their beaks, too."

"Well, um, they, they lay them the way God intended it to be."

Alicia rose an eyebrow. "And *how* do they do that? You've seen it happen, haven't you?"

"Of-of course, I did."

"Okay, then tell me."

"Well, they, uh, GOD! Yes. It's all done by God's will." She clapped her hands with pretended joy. "Oh, praise the Lord for his many, many miracles. The marvelous fruit of a wonderful bird! Oh, how *astounding*. So much is beyond our understanding."

Spoiled Alicia

Suspecting something being held off her, Alicia got upset. She asked, slowly, "The *fruit* of a bird?"

"Brilliantly said, my lady, *brilliantly said*. You're absolutely right. The fruit of a bird. Oh, *beautiful*—and in so many wonderful ways. Yes, it truly is."

"Mrs. Wagner," Alicia toyed with the Fabergé egg, rolling it back and forth under her finger, "I know where fruit comes from. I've seen trees. I've seen their flowers bloom. And I've seen their fruit grow." She shot Mrs. Wagner with a side-glare. "But I don't recall ever seeing flowers *bloom* on a bird."

"Why, of course not. It was only poetic imagery."

"But I didn't ask for poetry, now did I?" She stood up, grabbed the Fabergé egg, and approached Mrs. Wagner with it. "I asked you: How. Do chickens. Make eggs? And how do they lay them for us?"

Seeing where this was going, Mrs. Wagner was cornered. The reading-maids' glares were also upon her. One maid behind Alicia's back secretly mouthed *"Don't"*

"My lady, *please*. I'm sure someone else can explain it better."

"Answer me!"

"Well, they, they make them in-in… Inside of them."

"INSIDE THEM?" Alicia snapped.

"Lady Alicia—"

She raged, "How can something this big be made inside a creature so small? How can a small bird have this thing inside of it? You really expect me to believe that? Even if it's as big as a chicken, this thing is three times the size of its head! So how? Have you ever seen a chicken in your life?"

"Of course, I—"

"Is that why people are killing them? To get the eggs inside?"

"No, no, that's not—"

"Mrs. Wagner." Trembling with rage, Alicia hissed, "I'll ask you one last time: *how* do chickens lay eggs?"

Mrs. Wagner swallowed. "My lady, you see, what happens is, chickens do indeed make eggs inside of them, even two at a time sometimes, I'm not sure how, and then, and then, we get them."

"*Explain in detail.* NOW!"

"They, what they do is…"

"Yes?"

"They, they do chicken stuff. They do like this and, and this…" She tried to explain with body signals, "and they push and…"

Alicia watched Mrs. Wagner's comical show: how she

Spoiled Alicia

waved her arms like a chicken, bent up and down, until she, finally, touched her behind and acted as if she grabbed an egg falling from back there before she offered it to Alicia with a creepy smile.

Horror-stricken, Alicia froze.

The Fabergé egg dropped from her hand, and her eyes were so wide, it looked like they were about to pop out of her head…

It was said that the scream Alicia bellowed that night was heard in every corner of Füssen and the surrounding villages.

* * *

"WHAT HAVE YOU PEOPLE BEEN FEEDING ME?" Alicia raged, slamming her palm to the table. An egg was set in a golden cup in front of her.

Madam Schneider, Mr. Meyer, and Mr. Lang stood in one line across the table—Mr. Weber in his sleeping shirt and nightcap, half-asleep. He whispered to Mr. Meyer, "Is that an egg?"

He whispered back, "It looks like an egg."

"What is wrong with it?"

"I'm not sure."

"Why are we here?" whispered a sleepy Mr. Lang.

Madam Schneider said with the same secrecy, "I have a feeling we've got a problem."

Mr. Weber took a step forward and cleared his throat. "Lady Alicia, if I may ask, what seems to be the problem?"

"You're looking at it!"

"Is the egg bad?" He addressed a maid, "You, go replace it immediately."

Alicia raged, "It's not just bad, it's the worst thing in the world! Do you not know where this egg came from?"

"The kitchen...? A basket...? A chicken?"

"*A chickennn.*" Alicia hissed, fists balled, glaring at him with eyes of fire. "And how do chickens lay eggs, *hmm*?"

"Ah!" Mr. Weber figured it out. He looked at the rest from over his shoulder and whispered, "*We've got a problem.*"

Mr. Weber then turned to Alicia again and explained, "Lady Alicia, as I'm sure you already know, people don't eat the whole egg, only what's inside the shell, so you see, it's perfectly fine. It's a very, very clean and wonderful food."

"This thing you call *clean* was submersed in *gut* and *feces* before it was delivered to my lips straight out of the *rear* OF AN ANIMAL!"

"A bird, actually."

Spoiled Alicia

"I DON'T CARE WHICH!"

"It has a shell. It's impenetrable."

Alicia motioned with her head to the maid standing next to her, who shattered the raw egg with a spoon.

Mr. Weber said after a pause, "Well, we make sure the ones we serve you are."

At Alicia's signal, the maid grabbed a piece of the shell with a kerchief and approached the gathering with it. She was clearly trying not to laugh as she exhibited the broken piece close to their faces with a fake frown on her face—as Alicia spoke from behind the table.

"*This*, you see this? This fragile thing that can't even stand the poke of a finger is all that stands between *my food* and another creature's *waste*. A food you expect me to take into *my own body*."

Mr. Weber waved the maid from in front of him. "My lady, I understand your concerns, but I promise you, the shell is—"

"Even if what you say is true," she interrupted, pulling a piece of her dress in her hand, "you see this dress I'm wearing? If *this dress* was in a solid, perfectly secure box, submerged in animal waste. A *filthy, disgusting, smelly, animal waste*, would you still expect me to wear it? How then do you expect a human being made in the image of God to take such,

such, *filth*, such, *violation of nature,* into their temple…?"

She inhaled a deep breath through her nose, straightened her back, and said strongly, "Mr. Weber, this is no laughing matter. I expect you all to behave in accordance to your positions and address this issue with the seriousness it demands."

Giving up, Mr. Weber nodded his head hard. "You want us to ban eating eggs."

"I want you to ban eating eggs."

"In all the land?"

"In all the land."

"Done."

* * *

"Your services are no longer needed!" Madam Schneider yelled as she slammed the castle door shut in Mrs. Wagner's face.

Chapter 5

Alicia & Playmate

"Good morning, Mr. Kunibert."

Olga greeted a very gloomy Mr. Kunibert who sat on a box in front of his shop with his cheek glued to his palm. He was feeling so bad, he didn't find it in himself to return her greeting with more than a turn of his head.

"What's wrong?" Olga asked.

He sighed. "Haven't you heard? The castle banned butchering and eating chicken yesterday. I'm out of business."

"Yes, I've heard. Any idea why?"

"No one knows. Some say the castle suspects the chickens are sick, but I haven't heard of anyone getting sick after eating my chickens or anyone else's chickens."

"I'm sure they must have a very good reason." She summoned a smile and tried to cheer him up. "Well, look at the bright side, you will now steadily have more and more eggs to sell, so it's fine."

Mr. Kunibert buried his face in his palm and wept. "I

can't."

"Why not?"

"A messenger came from the castle this morning. They banned eggs, too."

"What?"

"It's true. Not only can I no longer sell them, but I can also get punished for as much as displaying them, gifting them, or even eating them myself."

Confused, Olga turned her gaze towards the castle for a little pause and back to Mr. Kunibert.

"Well, like I said, I'm sure they must have a very good reason, just as I'm sure it's only temporary," she said with a smile and handed him a brick of butter. "A gift."

"Thank you."

"Cheer up, Mr. Kunibert. Don't worry, I'll make sure you and Mrs. Kunibert will always have butter on your table every morning. Even if this drags longer, you can always pay me later."

"You're so kind."

She teased, "You still hope Alicia will come down here, don't you? That's what your *reliable source* said? Well then, when she does, you can complain to her about this."

"She was here," he said. "Spoiled Alicia. I saw her. She

stood right there in front of my store."

"No, I heard it was someone else. Some noble's daughter, traveling."

"I don't know. Maybe you're right. The people thought it was her and called her *Alicia*. Anyway, before I could talk to whoever she was, she collapsed. They say the poor thing is too fragile and couldn't stand the sun."

"Well, let's hope she's all right. If it was indeed Alicia, then I'm sure she will be back."

"If she does—"

Olga cracked a laugh. "I was joking! You really haven't given up, have you? Your promised gift will be fatter by then, or something?"

"Oh, not only that," he promised, "I'll show her how I can prepare three chickens with one blow."

"Impressive."

* * *

Mr. Weber was still asleep when a servant rushed into the room and woke him up.

"Sir… Sir."

Mr. Weber jolted. "What? What is it? What?"

When he saw who it was that shook him awake, Mr.

Weber lay back in bed and covered his face with his palm. "Good God. What is it, so early in the morning? I didn't get any sleep last night."

"I'm sorry, but I have urgent news."

"Fine, just, don't speak so loud, okay?"

The servant leaned to whisper the news in Mr. Weber's ear. As Mr. Weber listened, the sleep and tiredness were washed from his body. He shot up with a hard expression on his face.

"Go. Wake up my daughter."

"Sir?"

Angry, he threw the sheets off himself. "Tell her to wear her finest dress and meet me in the living room, immediately. This can't wait."

* * *

"Hurry, hurry," Mr. Weber rushed his daughter to follow him down the coach as they arrived at the stairs of the castle.

He was in such a hurry that he stopped halfway between the stairs and the coach, spinning around himself, as his fifteen-year-old daughter was yet at the door, pulling up the

Spoiled Alicia

ends of her dress, to step down.

Mr. Weber could not wait any longer. He rushed into the castle without her and headed straight to the main court where he saw Mr. Meyer, Mr. Lang, and an impressive young man he didn't recognize with blond hair and a sharp jaw, dressed in fancy polished armor for no apparent reason. The three men argued quietly about something.

"Mr. Meyer!" he called aloud as he hurried towards them.

"Mr. Weber? How surprising to see you here so early in the morning."

"I bet you are," he hissed to himself. As soon as he reached Mr. Meyer, he said, "I must say that I am utterly shocked by what I've heard. I had thought that such slithering in the shadows was underneath you, but I was clearly mistaken. You have truly disappointed my trust in you."

Mr. Meyer faced him, feigning ignorance. "I'm afraid I don't know what you mean."

"Don't you dare play such lowly games with me," Mr. Weber warned. He then hissed more quietly, "Trying to pick the rose for yourself before it even blossoms, eh? I am truly disappointed in you. When the lord hears about this—"

"The lord, Mr. Weber, will be most appreciative of my

concern for the young lady," Mr. Meyer interrupted. "I don't know what false rumors you may have heard, but I assure you there are no ill agendas at play here."

Mr. Weber raged, "Then what is it that I've heard about allowing yourself to appoint Princess Alicia a *personal bodyguard* without consulting me or any of the council members?"

"An act of *necessity* that has forced itself into play by unforeseen, unfortunate developments," Mr. Meyer responded coldly. "Following yesterday's incident and in light of the council's lack of action and Mr. Lang's failure in securing our princess's safety—"

Mr. Lang growled, "What failure?"

Mr. Meyer continued, uninterrupted, "I have taken it upon myself to resort to more assertive actions, as mere *precaution,* of course, to ensure that such incident never happen again."

"You dare accuse *me* of incompetence?" said Mr. Lang.

"You said it yourself that she hurt her head under your watch, didn't you? So, yes, unfortunately."

Mr. Weber hissed, "Such position cannot be created out of thin air without the council's approval, much less approve someone *all on your own* to fill it."

Spoiled Alicia

Not breaking eye contact with Mr. Weber, Mr. Meyer grabbed the young man by his upper arm and pulled him forth to introduce him.

"Alan, here, is my nephew. A brilliant mind, a brave soldier, and the lord's future bannerman. His trustworthiness is beyond question."

"Ah! Indeed. Indeed," Mr. Weber bellowed sarcastically, taking long strides towards Alan and patting his shoulders. "What a fine young man. A truly *fine* young man. Dressed to charm, I must say, *eh*? So, tell me—Mr. Brilliant Mind, Brave Soldier, and All of That—aside from our lady's safety, what else does the Meyer family have install for us, hm? *A walk* with Lady Alicia in the rose gardens? A private talk here and there, perhaps? *Ruffle* an innocent, inexperienced young heart with a charming smile, and before anyone knows it, it will be just the two of you on *a picnic* together, rowing on the same boat?"

Mr. Meyer hissed, faking insult, "*Most preposterous.* What exactly are you implying?"

"Exactly what you've heard." Mr. Weber stood in front of Mr. Meyer, glaring at him. "If there is, indeed, a need for a personal bodyguard for Lady Alicia, then *I* must be involved in making that decision, and a more suitable candidate with affirmed fixed intentions shall be chosen."

Mr. Lang could take this no longer. "Do I need to remind both of you that I am the Commander of the Guards of this castle?"

Mr. Weber dismissed it. "You *shut uuup*! If you had done your job properly, we wouldn't be in this mess right now."

"You are councilors!" Mr. Lang yelled. "Only *two* members of a council of ten, and neither of you is even the head of it. The rest of the council are with the lord. Meanwhile, it is clear that in the absence of our lord, Princess Alicia's safety is the highest priority. As Commander of the Guards, that responsibility is *mine*. I alone get to decide how and by whom this mission is carried out."

Mr. Meyer countered, "And we've seen it for ourselves how well you've been fulfilling that responsibility, haven't we?"

"Don't you dare question my abilities!"

"What is going on in here?" Madam Schneider approached them. "What's all the noise?"

Mr. Weber singled out Mr. Meyer with his hand. "This *concerned councilor* has decided all on his own to appoint Lady Alicia a *personal bodyguard* without consulting the rest of us."

"What?" Madam Schneider spat.

"His own nephew, of all people."

Spoiled Alicia

"Without my advisory as head of her maids? Most outrageous."

Mr. Meyer, hands joined at his chest, took a few steps from them and said haughtily, "It seems my intuition was correct from the beginning. It is just as I have feared." He spun on his heel to face them. "This is not just a matter of Lady Alicia's safety. Otherwise, I would've been content with a simple measure of increasing her security. No. None of you is able to grasp the depth of the real issue at hand."

Mr. Weber hissed, waving his hand, "And what is *the real issue at hand*? Please do enlighten us."

"It has been but a little over a day since our lord departed," Mr. Meyer explained, "and yet, the people have already lost both the chicken and the egg. A grave loss. Disastrous failure. I doubt the lord will let such a thing be swept under the rug, unpunished. And who knows what other disasters might happen before his return, if the status quo remains unchanged...? Now, I have been thinking about that all night long, and I've come to the conclusion that Lady Alicia's actions were driven by simple *insecurity*. The sudden loss of a protective, guiding, dependable fatherly figure has caused her to panic and, thus, act irrationally. That is where my nephew, Mr. Alan, comes in. Trust that I have chosen him after much consideration as he, undoubtedly, possesses all the requirements needed to fill the gap and restore peace into Lady Alicia's heart, which will quench any future mishaps before it occurs."

"What a coincidence!" Mr. Weber bellowed, smiling widely, taking comically long strides towards Mr. Meyer. "I, too, just so happen to have been thinking about the exact same thing, *all night long.*"

"Have you?"

"Yesss," he assured his fellow councilor with a big smile and wild nodding of his head, "and I have come to the same conclusion as well. It seems that great minds do think alike after all."

"So, you agree?" said Mr. Meyer.

"Without a doubt. That is why," Mr. Weber gestured toward his daughter, who was standing at the entrance of the court, "I've brought my daughter, Antoinette, to be Lady Alicia's *playmate.*"

Mr. Meyer frowned, his eyes wide with anger. "Her playmate?"

"Of course. Unlike a *personal bodyguard*—noble as your gesture may be—we don't need to go through any complicated procedures to choose a playmate for our lady, do we?"

Spoiled Alicia

Before Mr. Meyer could open his mouth, Mr. Weber answered for himself, "Of course not! As they will be simply *friends*." He then leaned into Mr. Meyer's face, mocking, "*Great friends*. Entrusted with each other's secrets, and the first to call for advice… And why wouldn't they be? They're both young ladies of the same age, same passions, same affinity. Trust that Antoinette will easily fill the gap you spoke of as she will guide, advise, and even introduce Lady Alicia to aspects of this world she had never immersed in without her having to take a step out of this castle. Thus, keeping her safe and out of trouble."

Madam Schneider jumped in, "Again, without my advisory? Shouldn't I at least see for myself if that young lady qualifies? And why would Lady Alicia need a playmate when she already has a dozen play-maids and twice as many for comfort and guidance? This can only upset the balance of her daily life."

"*Well*, one more fresh face can't hurt, can it?" Mr. Weber said.

Madam Schneider frowned. "You two haven't got a clue what you're getting yourselves into, do you? Very well. I'll let you find out for yourselves; now, if you would excuse me, I have a mistress to attend to." she turned on her heel and left, throwing over her shoulder, "And work out your stupid differences, it's getting ridiculous."

Mr. Weber grinned in Mr. Meyer's face. "I hope I didn't ruin any *plans* I wasn't aware of, did I?"

Mr. Meyer said, faking a smile and inhaling fire into his lungs, "We shall see about that. Ultimately, it is Lady Alicia's choice whether she would like the company of a reliable bodyguard or a *child playmate*."

"Ultimately."

They glared into each other's eyes for a short pause.

The smiles on their faces steadily vanished, and their faces hardened as they both reached the same conclusion about what should be done next.

Suddenly, they both raced to the stairs, with Mr. Meyer calling his nephew and Mr. Weber calling his daughter to follow.

* * *

The four of them raced for who would reach Alicia first.

Halfway through the tower's stairs, Mr. Weber stopped, panting for air with one hand on his chest, the other to the rails.

Out of breath, he told his daughter, Antoinette, who

had stopped to check on him, "Go. Go on without me."

"Yes."

He called after her, "Don't let that snake beat you. Go."

Mr. Meyer and his nephew reached Alicia's room first, Antoinette just a few steps behind. But Alicia wasn't there, just a handful of maids tending to the room and replacing rugs and sheets.

Mr. Meyer said, panting, "Where is she?"

"Our lady is not here," a maid said.

"Where?"

"She's taking her bath downstairs, the bath near the west entrance."

Sucking a great breath, Mr. Meyer and the other two raced down the stairs.

When he saw his daughter return, Mr. Weber, out of breath, asked, "Where are you going?"

"She's not there," Antoinette said as she scurried past him.

"What?"

"She's not there. She's downstairs."

Mr. Weber huffed in agony and followed them down as fast as he could.

* * *

Alicia was half-submerged in precious oils and hot water in an engraved marble tub laid next to a great open balcony that oversaw her rose gardens.

Suddenly, the door flew open as Mr. Weber, Mr. Meyer, Alan, and Antoinette barged in together.

The female performers stopped playing their instruments and stared at the new arrivals with widened eyes. Alicia's bathing-maids screamed with shock and hurried to hold up towels around the tub, lest the men see their mistress in nothing but her thin bathing shirt.

"What are you men doing? Get out of here!" a maid screamed.

The invaders spoke all together, their words tumbling out in a breathless jumble. "Princess Alicia—"

"Good morning, my lady—"

"What a wonderful day! This is Alan, my nephew—"

"The flowers and the stars—"

"My daughter—"

"Pleasure to meet you—"

Between the bathing-maids' inquiries and anger and the four arrivals' blubbering, no one could understand a thing being said.

Spoiled Alicia

A bathing-maid made a stand, putting herself between them and Alicia's bath with a brush in her closed fist. "Will you people stop talking all at once? What is this? Who allowed you in here?"

Once the hype went down, Alicia asked from behind the towels, "What's going on?"

"Princess Alicia," Mr. Meyer started, still gulping air. He received a slap to the side from Mr. Weber, who was holding his knees and sucking lungsful of air. He slapped Mr. Weber back and resumed, "I came to wish you good morning."

"Good morning."

"Thank you, *huff*, you are so kind. Also, also, I would like you to meet my nephew, Alan. After he heard about what happened in town yesterday, and out of his concern for you, he begged to be allowed by your side, as your personal bodyguard, to keep you from harm."

"Lady Alicia," Mr. Weber jumped in, still out of breath, but speaking as loudly as he could, "what a wonderful morning this truly is, to be able to hear your voice, and birds singing. What a beauty. What music. My lady, I'd like you to meet my daughter, Antoinette. When she heard about the great things, the truly great things you've done yesterday—"

Antoinette whispered, "What things?"

Mr. Weber poked her side with his elbow to shut up, he

resumed, "When she heard, she admired you so much, she insisted that she must meet you no matter what, to learn from your example and share so many wonderful, wonderful life experiences together, as I'm sure you two will."

Alicia said from her tub, "Oh, okay...... Does it have to be now?"

A bathing-maid gritted her teeth. "Will the men in this room *please* get out, so the lady can have her bath in peace?"

Mr. Meyer and Alan froze, where as Mr. Weber's face brightened suddenly.

Smiling widely, Mr. Weber said, "Ahh! Indeed. We, *men*, as in, the three of us, *must* leave."

"If you *please*," the bathing-maid hissed with impatience.

He wrapped his arms around the other two. "Of course. How careless of us! Wouldn't you agree, Mr. Meyer? We made a terrible mistake. We should've been more considerate of the lady's privacy before we barged in like that."

Mr. Meyer muttered, "Apparently."

"Excellent." Mr. Weber steered the two men towards the door. He said to the bathing-maid, "Please forgive us. We'll be on our way now, and sorry for the interruption."

"Just hurry out and LEAVE."

Mr. Weber paused near the door to whisper to

Spoiled Alicia

Antoinette, "Remember what we talked about: *best. Friends. No matter what.*"

Once the men had left and the door had closed, the bathing-maids lowered the towel. Whispers of shock and contempt rumbled all over the place.

Antoinette turned and saw Alicia in the tub.

"Who are you?" Alicia asked.

Antoinette summoned a smile and curtsied. "Good morning, my lady. I am Antoinette, Mr. Weber's daughter."

"Oh, good morning."

"I've heard so much about you." She came closer and stood at the foot of Alicia's tub. "My father always thought we should get together some time and be introduced properly. You know, get to know each other a little more. He believes I have much to learn from you, and so do I. So, here I am."

"Sure. What do you wish to learn?"

She giggled and seated herself on the rim of the tub. "I don't know, it doesn't have to be learning. It can be anything. You know, we can just talk, spend time together, play together—all the experiences we could have. It can be anything you want." She winked. "Don't you want us to be friends?"

Alicia smiled sweetly back. "Of course."

Antoinette giggled. "Wonderful. Best friends forever?" She was about to reach out with her pinky to Alicia when Alicia slowly raised her foot towards Antoinette from underneath the water.

Antoinette paused, confused. Before she could say anything, a bathing-maid put a brush in her hands.

Clueless, she looked at Alicia while waving the brush and asked humorously, "What?"

"It's okay," Alicia assured her, "I permit it."

One bathing-maid secretly mouthed, *"Brush,"* while another, who stood behind Alicia, made a scrubbing motion with her hands, signaling Antoinette to brush the bottom of Alicia's foot.

Turning her face between the brush and Alicia, Antoinette faked a giggle, a creepy smile on her face.

* * *

Down in the castle's main court, Mr. Weber walked back and forth, hands joined behind his back, mocking Mr. Meyer with his indirect hints.

"Oh my, they've been together for *sooo looong*. Young women, they truly have no sense of time when they're having fun."

Mr. Meyer gritted his teeth. "It's only been an hour."

"And who knows how much longer will we be waiting, eh? I'm telling you, friendship these days, once a bond is formed, it's next to impossible to break. Who knows what joyful tales they could be sharing? What little girls' secrets they're whispering? What advices, warnings about *deceptive men* could they be learning from one another?"

Mr. Weber then approached Mr. Meyer and threw his arm around Mr. Meyer's shoulders like a good old friend.

"I've got to tell you," Mr. Weber continued, "this approach you suggested is working *splendidly*. I can already feel it. These two young ladies will be nothing but good influences on each other."

Suddenly, they heard footsteps hurrying down the stairs and the sound of Antoinette crying. Mr. Weber turned towards his daughter with worry.

"*Fatherrr…*" Antoinette threw herself in Mr. Weber's arms, crying her heart out.

"Darling, what happened? Are you all right? Is Alicia all right?"

The fifteen-year-old looked up at him and said, half-hysterical, her cheeks glistening with tears, "I want to go home—"

"What—"

"I don't like it here. I don't want to do this. I want to go home now!"

"Antoinette, what happened? Talk to me."

"It was terrible! I can't do this, I can't. Father, you must get me out of here, *please*."

He shook her, almost yelling, "Antoinette, pull yourself together, tell me what the hell happened."

Antoinette explained, the best she could, "She, after you left, she made me bathe her, and I had to scrub, and I had to massage her feet, and perfume her toes, and then, and then, she made me do things, *horrible, humiliating things*, Father, I can't say it, the things she made me *dooo…* I couldn't stand it, but I did as you told me, I did everything that I could for her, but she kept saying I was doing it all wrong. Nothing could make her happy, *nothing…*! And I endured it, I really, really endured it with all that I've got, but then, she, she—"

She burst into heartful crying and could not finish.

Mr. Weber tried to calm her down with a soothing tone, a pretended laugh, and a hug. "*Darling*, it's okay, it's all right, you're exaggerating. So, she asked you to help her with her bath and a few things, what's the big deal? That's what best friends do, right?"

Spoiled Alicia

Antoinette cried with hysteria, throwing her little fists at his chest. "Father, you don't understand! She, she took me to her, her private chamber, and made me watch, she made me watch while she... while she did *her thiiing.*"

"What, private chamber? What thing? OHH...!" His eyes widen with shock as it suddenly dawned on him what Antoinette meant.

She buried her face in his chest and howled with shame, "And I had to stand there *the whole tiiime.*"

"What-what about her private-maids? Why weren't they there, doing their job?"

"They *weeeere...*" she whined. "We were all in there together. Everyone was there. EVERYONE! The whole town will hear about this!" She cried some more. "And then, and then, she told me that she wanted to give me a gift—"

"Well, uh, a gift? That's good, that's good."

"—She said, that, that, for our new friendship, I got to have the honor, and told her maid to let me have the kerchiefs. And I just stood there holding the kerchiefs in my hands, not knowing what she meant. And then, and then, she stood up, and bent over, and I had to, had to, *wiippeee...* to the sound of *muuusic.*"

Stunned speechless. Mr. Weber didn't know what to say as his daughter howled and cried her heart out into his chest.

"I want to leave."

"Yes."

"I want to go home. I don't want to remember any of this."

"Yes, yes." Mr. Weber held her by her forearms and said, "It's all right, love, you did what you could. You did well. Go home now, take the coach and go back home. I will follow you soon."

Antoinette ran to the door, crying aloud and not seeing a thing in her way.

He called after her, "Don't tell your mother!"

Mr. Meyer stared mockingly at Mr. Weber, who froze, motionless with shock.

"I... I didn't know about that," Mr. Weber muttered.

"What a pity," Mr. Meyer taunted. "I was looking forward to Miss. Antoinette's positive influence on Lady Alicia."

Mr. Weber grunted with rage.

"Oh well," Mr. Meyer laughed, "now that the playmate option is no longer available, I guess we have no alternative but to put our hopes on *my choice*."

Chapter 6

Alicia & Bodyguard

Alicia came down the stairs with some of her maids and gazed around. "Where is Antoinette? She told me she would meet me here."

Mr. Weber replied, "I'm afraid she wasn't feeling well. I had to send her home."

"Goodness, is she all right?" she asked as her little palm flew to her chest with genuine concern.

"Yes, I'm sure she will be, once she has rested properly."

"Oh, I sincerely hope so," Alicia said. "I was looking forward to play with her. We barely got to know each other."

"My apologies, she's very fragile. Her stamina let her down."

Mr. Meyer commented, "If only Mr. Weber had twenty-four daughters, they might have lasted a day."

Mr. Weber glared daggers at him. "But I'm sure she's looking forward to the opportunity, at a future date."

"Me too," said Alicia. "Let her know that my thoughts

are with her."

"I will. Thank you."

"In the meantime," Mr. Meyer extended his arm for his nephew, Alan, who proudly stepped forth in his shiny armor and bowed, "if my lady would be so kind as to allow me to introduce Mr. Alan, again."

"Pleasure," Alan said.

Mr. Weber approached them and tried to interfere, "I'm sure this can wait—*aghh*!"

"I'm sure it cannot," Mr. Meyer said after swiftly and secretly twisting Mr. Weber's finger behind his back. He addressed Alicia, "We were so concerned after yesterday's unfortunate incident, we determined it *essential* that a personal bodyguard be appointed for your person to prevent such misfortunes from ever happening again. The council had had its mind set on this for quite some time now, in fact. And, if I may add, it's only *fit* that a lady of your prestigious stature have one."

"Oh? Okay."

"Thank you for your approval. Now, if you would excuse us, Mr. Weber and I have some urgent matters to attend."

"No, we don't," Mr. Weber asserted.

Spoiled Alicia

"Yes, *we do*." Mr. Meyer twisted Mr. Weber's finger harder. "We have that important thing we must look into, remember? " He dragged Mr. Weber backwards by his finger. "Please excuse us. I'm sure you and Alan have much to talk about."

Mr. Weber whispered, "You sneaky little rat."

"I could say the same about you." Reaching the door, Mr. Meyer gave Mr. Weber a push, literally throwing him out of the hall and shutting the door on him.

Mr. Meyer said, "Oh, Mr. Alan, before I leave, can I have a word with you?"

"Excuse me, princess," Alan said with a bow.

Their backs to Alicia, Mr. Meyer discretely placed a gold necklace with an enormous diamond in Alan's hand.

"This is our family's treasure," he whispered. "The price of this diamond can feed Füssen *for a month*. Use it. You must not give her a chance to retaliate, start off with a decisive blow: the diamond, poetry, charm, and praise. There's not much time, I want this wrapped within a week, you understand?"

"Yes."

"Good. I'll keep Mr. Weber at bay."

As the old men were out of the scene, Alan approached Alicia with a charming smile. "Sorry about that, last-moment instructions and all."

"Of course. So, Mr. Alan—"

"Please, call me Alan."

Alan froze, confused, as before he could take Alicia's arm, a maid intercepted his hand with a frown on her face. Once Alicia motioned her approval, the maid put a kerchief over her mistress's forearm before allowing Alan's hand to land on it.

He chuckled. "Well, I see that your maids are...Quite dedicated."

"The best," she assured him.

Alan was even more confused when Alicia simply led the way to wherever she intended to go, instead of letting him take the lead.

"So, Alan, tell me: what exactly does a bodyguard do that other castle guards don't?"

"Well, um, for instance, the guards have places they must be at, things to do, patrols to commence, set orders to follow, whereas I will be close to you at all times. I'm assigned not to a certain place but to your own person."

"My person? Only?" she asked as she took her arm back and assumed a seat near a big window.

"Yes, specifically for your protection."

Spoiled Alicia

"Excellent, so you're like a maid in arms? I like it."

He stammered, "A maid—?"

"No, stand over there." She signaled him. "You're in the way of my cup-maid."

Making way for the maid who held Alicia's cup of posset, Alan went around to the other side of her seat.

"And what else do you do?" Alicia asked.

"I—"

"Move forward a little, the breeze is more precious."

Confused, he looked over his shoulder and then back at her. "Breeze?"

She rolled her eyes. "You're blocking *the breeze*."

"Oh!"

"Why do you think I decided to sit here? I want to feel the breeze on my face."

"Yes, of course, sorry." He moved a step forward.

Summoning a charming smile, he started again, "So, um, as to your question, my lady, please never mind—"

"Mm, too warm, replace it," she said to her cup-maid, who watered her with a spoon.

Alan continued, as if uninterrupted, "Never mind what my duties are. They're numerous, and you'll get to know them with time. As for now," he put his hand behind his back and prepared his trump card, the diamond, "I have a gift for you."

Alicia suddenly snapped, almost hopping on her seat with joy, "GIFT?"

It worked!

With a boost to his confidence, Alan came down on one knee at the foot of her seat and said, with the low, charming voice of a lover, "Yes. A gift. You may not have known this, my beautiful princess, but I had seen you once before when I first came to the castle, and I thought to myself, oh, how you look better than a lake surrounded by roses."

Touched, Alicia's hands flew to her chest.

"Thus, when I heard of my new assignment, I just couldn't let this opportunity slip between my fingers without presenting you with a symbol of my affection." He produced the diamond before her eyes. "Please accept this jewel with a pledge of my ever faithfulness to *you*."

With an emotional "aww," she accepted it in the palms of her hands. "It's so pretty. I love it."

Alicia then quickly passed it to one of her maids and stared eagerly at Alan, her hands atop one another over her knee, a smile on her lips and a glitter in her eyes.

Alan was confused. There was something about the way Alicia looked that just screamed with eagerness. He just wasn't sure what she was expecting to hear next.

"My lady?"

She swiftly reached out her open palm to him and yelped with joy, "The other one."

"Other one?"

Bewildered, Alicia suspected she made a mistake. She drew her hand back. "Oh, that was it?"

He chuckled nervously. "What?"

"Oh, it's nothing." She raised her palm to the maid who put the diamond back in Alicia's hand. Her smile couldn't hide the disappointment in her tone. "It's… So lovely. Yes, lovely." She turned to her maids. "Lovely, don't you think?"

"Lovely."

"Lovely, my lady."

"You don't like it?" asked Alan.

"Nooo, of course I do. I love it. I love it, and it's very nice of you, and I will cherish it forever." She passed the diamond back to her maid.

Turning his face between Alicia and the maid who took her *cherished diamond*, Alan felt awkward. The maids, who were secretly stealing looks at him, were so amused, they were having a hard time restraining their laughter.

He asked, "What, *uhm*, if I may ask, what exactly was on your mind just now? You know, when you said—"

"Oh, that was nothing, really. It's just that, well, normally, how this kind of thing goes is that my father would always presents me the small diamond first, before he surprises me with the big one. I just, I kind of thought you were doing the same. You know: *surpriiise*!"

"Ah!"

"But it's fine, really, I mean, I understand that you're poor and struggling. I'm considerate to all of that—"

"Poor?"

"So, don't worry about it. I mean, I know you'll get me a real diamond, eventually," she said with a hopeful smile.

Alan stared at her blankly for a moment. He faked a chuckle and went for a different approach. "You like poetry?"

She clapped her hands with joy. "I *looove* poetry. How did you guess?"

* * *

"Ah! *Sprüing*," Mr. Meyer intoned as he brought a cup of wine to Mr. Weber, paying him back for all his sarcasm earlier, "what a wonderful season. Magical. It almost makes me feel like *falling in love* again."

Spoiled Alicia

Mr. Weber grunted, "Good. I'll make sure to pass a note to your wife."

Mr. Meyer sat across the table from him. "Too bad we're past that point, you and I. Not to worry, we can still have the joy of watching innocent young couples discovering the wonders of falling love for the first time."

"The only one you ever fell in love with was *your pouch*!"

Mr. Meyer turned comically towards the door. "They sure are taking their time. I wonder what could be keeping Lady Alicia and *Alan*?"

"Don't get your hopes up. It's only been half an hour." Mr. Weber huffed and jumped to his feet. "And it's long enough for *me* to make my return."

Mr. Meyer grabbed his hand, stopping him. "But do you really think we should intrude? A lot can happen in half an hour, you know. What if you interrupt Lady Alicia at a critical time? Oh, how upset she will be!"

"In your dreams. Now, get your filthy hands off me, you lousy little—"

"RATS!" Alan barged through the door, cursing and causing both men to freeze, stunned.

Mr. Meyer hurried after Alan, who scurried past them. "Wait, wait! Where are you going?"

"Anywhere but here!"

"What happened? Alan? Did you two get into an argument or something? Didn't she feel satisfied? What? Alan, there's a lordship at stake!"

Alan stopped to yell at Mr. Meyer, "Screw the lordship. Whoever can satisfy that-that-that *woman* DESERVES TO BE KING!"

"Alan? Alan, stop! The future of our family—"

"CAN GO TO HELL!" He slammed the door shut behind himself.

Stunned, both men turned around slowly, staring in awkward silence at the door, behind which Alicia was.

* * *

Hands joined before her, Madam Schneider entered the room and found Mr. Weber and Mr. Meyer at a table, drinking and singing a tavern's sad song together.

"It's good to see the two of you have worked out your differences."

Mr. Weber answered as he poured Mr. Meyer a drink, "It's not that hard, really, when both sides of the battle are crushed."

"I love my wife," said Mr. Meyer. "I never realized how

Spoiled Alicia

little I appreciated her. She's a saint. An angel!"

Madam Schneider rubbed the side of her temple. "I take it that your *idiotic* plans have failed. Well, not that I'm surprised, but care to tell me what happened?"

"Well," said Mr. Meyer, "his daughter is back home, probably crying herself to sleep, so that should answer your question."

"And his nephew is on his way to find a new life. Probably way out of town already."

"Your daughter didn't last an hour."

"Yours didn't last half that much."

"I see." She shrugged. "Well, I expected worse."

"Somehow, I just know that the worst is yet to come. And it hasn't even been two days since the lord left the castle." Mr. Weber looked up at her. "How did you do it *all these yeeeears*?"

"I conquer with numbers," Madam Schneider said firmly, stunning both men with her answer.

"Why else did you think lady Alicia has so many maids?" she said. "Not only do I need them fully staffed and at alert at any given moment, but I also need just as many ready at quick notice to replace those who can no longer work. I have a room in this castle for that purpose alone. My maids call it *the hall of tears*. Any maid who breaks down can go lock herself in there and cry 'till she pulls herself together."

They stared oddly at her.

She admitted, a hint of shame in her voice, "It…works best when they break down in a group. They can hug, cry together, and help each other back on their feet."

The men looked at one another, stunned.

A maid entered the room, hurrying on her toes, and whispered something to Madam Schneider.

"And it looks like our problems for today have only just started," said Madam Schneider. "Alicia plans on going to town again, as in: right now."

Panicked, the men jumped to their feet.

Chapter 7

Alicia & Peephole

Olga sat down on the grass at the edge of the farm, placed the small sack she had brought with her in her lap, rested her head on her palms, and watched Diedrich and another man pull a plough through dirt. Other men were farther away, doing the same.

No wonder Diedrich would return exhausted every evening. Pulling iron through the ground looked like a really tough job. But, for a moment, Olga wished it was tougher. The sight of her beloved's strained muscles and sweat-coated skin excited her. She couldn't take her eyes off him.

Olga didn't announce her arrival. Instead, she watched them quietly for a time until Diedrich noticed her. He exchanged a quick word with his friend, and both men agreed to take a short break.

Diedrich approached her, gulping water from a leather flask he picked off the ground as he walked. He then raised it overhead and let the water shower his head.

"I've brought you lunch," Olga said casually.

"Thanks." He sat beside her, panting with tiredness, his upper half soaked wet.

"How's work?"

"Halfway there... The remaining sections are flatter, it should be easier from now on."

"Good to hear."

He took the sack from her lap, set it on his, and opened it. "What did you bring me?"

"Ham, cheese, bread, and Mrs. Fischer gave me a bag of berries, I thought you'd like some."

"Oh, that's great."

Olga went quiet. She stared at him with a smile.

Diedrich was a hearty eater. She loved watching him eat. Her eyes feasted on her beloved as her gaze slowly dropped from his wet brown hair to the beads of water swiftly gliding down his unshaved cheek to his sharp jaw and the wet shirt adhering to his muscular white chest.

It got to her.

Feeling ticklish, Olga shifted her hips slightly from side to side over grass. She stole looks at the other men working on the farm to ensure no one was looking their way and made up her mind at the spot.

"*Pssttt.*" She nudged her beloved with her elbow. When

he looked at her, she naughtily bit on her lower lip and signaled him with her eyes towards the abandoned shabby cottage, not too far behind their backs.

He turned his face between her and the cottage and asked, clueless, "What?"

Olga rolled her eyes. How could he not get the hint?

She punched his upper arm suddenly and took off running, giggling, towards the cottage.

Diedrich finally figured it out. He threw a quick glance towards his friends, who had not noticed a thing, put the sack of food aside in a hurry and chased after her.

* * *

"I am one to admit my shortfalls," Alicia assured her councilors as she headed out to her coach. "Yesterday's trip was only a partial success."

Mr. Weber followed her. "Yes, exactly, a success. So, why the need to go down there again?"

With one foot on the coach's step, she looked at him from over her shoulder. "*Because* it was only a partial success."

Once inside, with the coach's door shut, one of Alicia's travel-maids—who were ordered to wear plain clothes—opened the window for her.

Alicia added, "I'll leave the coach and guards behind at a fair distance, to not attract attention like last time."

"Leave the guards behind?"

"That cannot be allowed. Lady Alicia, please be reasonable," said Mr. Meyer.

"Relax, I thought this over. My travel-maids will be with me, and they are dressed to blend in, as you saw."

"I must urge you to reconsider. The lord will be most displeased by the lack of security."

"I said don't worry, I'll be in and out of town in a heartbeat. I'm just going to take a quick peek at how my people are doing. What could possibly go wrong?"

"Wouldn't it be more sufficient to send spies instead?" said Mr. Meyer.

"Yes, spies, yes. Excellent suggestion," Mr. Weber affirmed. "Whatever you wish to know will be reported to you with immense detail. So, you see, there's really no need for all of this."

She grimaced. "I will not *spy* on my own people… Move out." She ordered her wagoner.

With dismayed faces, they watched Alicia leave.

Madam Schneider turned to return to the castle, throwing over her shoulder, "Why do I bother letting you useless lot know if you can't as much as influence a twelve-year-old mind…? I'll tell the doctors to be on standby."

* * *

On her way to Füssen again, intending to establish how her people were doing, Alicia watched with a smile as the natural scenes floated before her eyes.

Something caught her attention as they neared the town. She asked a travel-maid, "What are those people doing?"

The travel-maid looked through the window. "My lady, these are some of the town farmers. They're ploughing and preparing the land."

Narrowing her gaze, Alicia declared, "Stop the coach." She came down and said to Mr. Lang, "I won't be long."

"Let me accompany you, at least," begged Mr. Lang.

"No need. I'll be right there. It's just behind that line of trees."

"But—"

She silenced him before he could object. "Don't argue. And make sure that everyone keeps their distance." Alicia then signaled for two of her travel-maids with plain clothes. "You two, you're coming come with me."

With her travel-maids a step ahead, twisting the branches out of their mistress's way the best they could and warning Alicia of traitorous roots sticking out of the ground, the three women snuck through the vegetation and grass, away from the road.

They came to the edge of the farm.

"Look how pretty the view is," one maid said.

Alicia silenced her. "*Shush*. Did you hear that?"

"What?"

"Listen…" Alicia and her maids listened carefully. They soon caught wind of Olga's voice. "There. You hear? It sounds like someone is hurting."

"I hear it."

"It's coming from over there," one maid said, motioning towards the old cottage.

Living up to her stature, Alicia ordered, her face a frown of assertiveness in time of distress, "Go check it out, quickly. Someone might be in trouble."

The travel-maid rushed to take a look—at first. But the closer to the cottage she walked, the slower her steps, as it became clear *this* was not what they initially had thought.

When the maid reached the cottage, she hesitated. Her cheeks were warm with embarrassment already. She looked over her shoulder at Alicia and the other maid heading her way before she stole a peek through a hole in the wall.

Her eyes widened, and her cheeks turned pink.

"What's happening?" Alicia asked.

The travel-maid spun on her heel so quickly, her foot slid. She stood in front of the hole, waving her arms and speaking quietly. "Nothing, nothing, nothing. Everything is fine, my lady."

"Everything fine?" Alicia asked.

"Who was screaming?"

"No one. There is no one inside," she assured Alicia while signaling her friend with her eyes.

Alicia raised an eyebrow. "Why are you whispering?"

"I'm not. We, um, we just heard wrong."

The other maid said, "I was sure we heard someone."

Frustrated by her friend's thick headed, her fists balled as she glared at the other maid. "Do you not understand the words coming out of my mouth? I said, no one is *hurting*. Get it? Everything is *fiiine. Too fine.* There's *no need to look.*"

"Oh!" the other maid caught up. She addressed Alicia, "Yes, yes, everything is perfectly fine. My lady, this happens all the time, it means nothing. We, we should probably go back and—"

Olga let out such a vibrating moan, it sent the maids to

their toes with their hands covering their mouths in embarrassment.

Alicia hissed, "Everything is *fine*? That was a scream, just now. I heard it."

"No. I'm sure it wasn't."

"I didn't hear anything."

"The wind around these parts can make all kinds of noises, really, you should hear what it's like on a rainy day." She faked a giggle.

Not buying it, Alicia barged forth. "What's going on in there?"

Her travel-maids quickly intercepted her. "My lady, listen to me, there's nothing to look at, I swear."

"We need to go back now. My lady, *please*."

Alicia said, "You two might be scared, but *I* am not."

"We are scared."

"For a totally different reason."

"Out of my way."

"My lady, if you will please trust us."

Alicia was at her wits' end with them. She hissed with pure venom, "I said. Out. Of my way. Before I have the guards remove you."

The travel-maids looked at one another with dismay.

They cleared the path for Alicia, who stepped forward and peeked through the hole.

Alicia gasped. She whispered urgently, "Call the guards, quickly."

"My lady, we really shouldn't."

"Let's just leave them alone and pretend this never happened."

Shocked, Alicia raged, but still kept her voice down, "Leave them alone? That woman is in trouble."

"I'm sure she had it coming."

"She will manage."

"What? Manage? She's being attacked. Can't you hear how desperate she is?"

One maid buried her face in her palms. "Oh, I hear it."

The other nodded with bitter jealousy, "It's a level of despair I've never reached."

Alicia snapped, "What is wrong with you two? If we don't do something quickly, that man is going to kill her. Call the guards now. What are you still standing here for?"

The maids looked at one another. One of them motioned with her head towards Alicia, indicating they should explain it to her, but the other maid mouthed a "no."

"If you're too scared to take action, then I will." Alicia started towards the door.

Panicked, her maids stopped her. "No, no, no, no."

"My lady, you really mustn't intrude."

"Intrude?" Alicia yelped.

The maid wiped her face with her palm and sighed. She bent down to Alicia's level, fixed a loose lock of hair behind Alicia's ear, and said, "My lady, it's not what you think. What they're doing is, well…" She whispered the details.

Alicia listened attentively. The other maid joined them, occasionally whispering in Alicia's other ear, too.

"Aha… Aha… Make what?" Alicia asked. "What do babies got to do with… But how…? Aha… Aha… Aha… Poke her with what…? And where is that?"

Her eyes widened, and the color drained from Alicia's face as the picture became clear. She set her palms on her maids' shoulders and pushed them off herself.

"My lady?"

Alicia looked suddenly disoriented.

She stumbled in a random direction, panting for air, and set her hand on a tree for support.

She fainted…

* * *

Spoiled Alicia

Mr. Weber approached Mr. Lang and Mr. Meyer in the castle main court. He joined his hands behind his back and asked sarcastically, "Sooo, which dish are we taking off the menu today?"

"That's not funny," groused Mr. Lang.

"I was just asking, what happened this time? What animal did she discover how people cook? Please tell me it wasn't a pig, I beg you."

"It wasn't a pig, all right?" Mr. Lang snarled.

"There was no animal this time," Mr. Meyer assured him. "According to Mr. Lang and everyone involved, princess Alicia didn't even make it halfway to town."

Mr. Weber raised his arms to his sides. "What could possibly happen between here and the town? What, she just, *fainted*, for no reason? Was it the heat? The sun? What?"

"I'm sure there must be a reason," said Mr. Meyer, "but her maids refuse to say a word. We'll just have to wait and see."

* * *

Madam Schneider paced back and forth in front of Alicia's room, deeply distraught and wringing her hands nervously.

"I should not have allowed her to go. This is my fault. I should not have allowed her to go," she kept repeating to herself.

A doctor tried to bring ease to her chest. "Madam Schneider, if you'd please calm down. I'm confidant she will wake up very soon."

Suddenly, they heard Alicia scream with horror.

Madam Schneider barged into Alicia's room with a swarm of nursing-maids and doctors, inquiring about how Alicia was doing.

They found Alicia cowering by the headboard of her bed, her hands clutching a pillow to her chest and her eyes darting everywhere like a terrified cat.

A maid asked quietly, "Princess Alicia…?"

With her chest heaving in and out, Alicia hissed with rage, "Open the armory. *Arm all maids.*"

Chapter 8

Alicia & the Devil

The next morning, Mr. Weber marched through the entrance to the castle's main court in a hurry, raising his voice with joy.

"Ah! Princess Alicia, what a joy to the heart to see you've recovered from misfortune. What a joy indeed. The birds and heavens above are filled with—"

"Hold it right there!" a maid intercepted him, ten paces away from her mistress.

He froze, confused. "What?" He regained his smile and went around the maid. "Princess—"

The maid jumped in his way, her eyes ferocious and her voice growling. "I said hold it right there! Not a step closer."

"Excuse me?"

"For your mistress's own safety, you will comply like a good subject and keep distance from her ladyship at all times, *understood*?"

Overtaken by awkwardness, Mr. Weber eyed at the maid up and down. "And who are you to give *me* orders?"

"Charlette here is my new maid. I'd do as she says, if I were you," Alicia replied calmly.

He humored, "Hah, a distancing-maid?"

"Close combat."

His eyes widened. Charlette set the palm of her hand on the flintlock pistol, tucked in her white belt, and slowly cracked the hammer back with her thumb.

Mr. Weber retreated a couple steps back.

He turned his gaze from the maid to the rest of the room as he noticed the lack of castle guards, the unusual number of maids present, and all their weapons.

"Pssttt…"

Mr. Weber turned his face towards the sound and saw that all the—male—officials of the court, Mr. Lang and Mr. Meyer included, had gathered in one corner of the hall.

Mr. Meyer signaled him. "Over here."

Mr. Weber joined them. He whispered very quietly, "What's going on? Where are the guards? And why are all the maids in arms?"

"I haven't got a clue," Mr. Meyer whispered back.

Mr. Lang said, "I hate to bring it to you, Mr. Weber, but it seems that the maids are, in effect, in control of the castle."

He stared at him. "Is this a joke?"

"Do you see any of my men around?"

"You tell me that your men *conceded*, overnight, to eight hundred *maids*? What did they do, polish your men's armor to submission? Tickle their noses with feather dusters? Just when I thought you couldn't possibly be any more incompetent than you already were. You have truly outperformed yourself, Mr. Lang."

Mr. Lang grimaced. "It was Lady Alicia's *orders*. She *ordered* all guards disarmed and reassigned to outer perimeters, beyond the castle's walls. There was nothing I could do." He faced forward, then added, "Cooks and gardeners, too. We were all out there. Myself included."

"Doing what, exactly?"

"Improvising tents. It was pretty cold… We slept closely together."

Mr. Meyer said, "And if I may add to Mr. Lang's earlier statement, they're not eight hundred anymore."

"What?" Mr. Weber looked at him.

"I've heard there's an active recruiting process going on as we speak. And not just in Füssen but in all surrounding villages, too. The intent is to hire two thousand more, minimum."

His eyes wide, Mr. Weber asked, "Two thousand? And who will shoulder the financial burden to all of this? This is ridiculous. Where is Madam Schneider?"

"I haven't seen her since yesterday noon," said Mr. Lang.

"Are we sure this isn't April's fool thing?"

"We're not in April yet, Mr. Weber," said Mr. Meyer. "We were waiting for you. It seems Lady Alicia has an announcement to make."

"Well, I hope it explains something."

They saw Madam Schneider arrive. She stopped by the men and said under her breath, "I did all that I could for you... I'm sorry."

"Sorry?"

"Sorry for what?"

Madam Schneider didn't answer. She continued her way down the court, where she stood at Alicia's wing.

Feeling awkward, Mr. Weber whispered, "Mr. Meyer, not that it's any of my business, but why are you getting executed?"

"Of course I'm not, stupid. What for?"

Alicia cleared her voice, gaining everyone's attention.

"I'm glad you're all here... Now, it has come to my attention that an *unspeakable evil* resides in this world. One that cannot, and should not, be trusted. One that I cannot bring myself to ignore." She narrowed her gaze and hissed, glaring at the men, "One that resides *in yoouuu*... And while your loyalty and good intentions are well established through years of good service, as Madam Schneider repeatedly assured me, I'm afraid that's just not going to be enough to restore the trust I once had in you."

The men looked at one another, clueless.

Mr. Meyer, eyes darting left and right at the men around him, leaned at Mr. Weber to whisper, "Who do you think the traitor is?"

Mr. Weber poked him with his elbow. He then took a step forward.

"Lady Alicia, it seems I'm missing something. What evil are you speaking of, exactly?"

She hissed, breathing fire on her lips, "I am speaking of *the devil's horn* each of you has."

Stunned silence…

"Ah!" Mr. Weber made his escape, "I'm going home." He whispered.

Mr. Meyer stopped him by the elbow. "The hell you are."

Mr. Weber whispered back, "Look, I haven't even had *the talk* with my own daughter yet, but I'm sure you'll do just fine."

"*You* are not moving a step from here until we sort this out."

"Why should I be the one to sort it out? Speak to Lang. He caused this. Let him fix it."

Mr. Lang raged, his voice low, "How did I cause this?"

"Well, unless she found the *devil's horn* laying around in her coach then, obviously, it must be your fault."

Mr. Meyer affirmed, "It does seem that every time Lady Alicia leaves the castle with you, she ends up exposed to something bad."

"*Exposed?*" Mr. Lang yelped. "How dare you! What kind of a man do you think I am?"

"That's what we want to know. What exactly did you do out there?"

Alicia raised her voice, "Are you done whispering?" The men stiffened at attention. She motioned at them with her head, her young face maimed with disgust. "What have you got to say for yourselves? Or should I ask: *what* were you planning to do with it?"

More awkward silence…

Mr. Meyer pushed Mr. Weber forward. "Mr. Weber will explain."

Mr. Meyer then tried to exit the room, but Mr. Weber

grabbed him before he could escape. "You're not pinning this on me, you cowardly snake."

"If you've got nothing to say," Alicia declared, "then I am ready to issue my decree: As of this moment, and until a more permanent solution will be found, all guards are to remain disarmed and conduct their duties strictly at the outer perimeter, outside the castle. Those who will be permitted to enter will be under constant monitor for the duration of their stay—and even then—I want every, single, person infected with this-this *extension*, this, *abomination of God's image* to maintain ten paces from every woman in the castle at all times, under penalty of imprisonment *or worse*."

The men's faces paled with worry.

"Permanente...?"

* * *

Mr. Weber, Mr. Meyer and Mr. Lang chased after Madam Schneider as she hurried down the corridor, refusing to stop.

"Madam Schneider—"

"Ten paces, Mr. Weber. Or the ladies following you will start shooting."

"A—what?" Stunned, he looked over his shoulder at

the armed maids trailing them.

Mr. Lang said, "Look, we are keeping ten paces. Now, can you please stop for a moment?"

"Madam Schneider, *please*."

"Out of the question," she said.

"Let us talk about this."

"There is nothing to talk about. I already told you, I've done everything that I can for you."

"And we can all see where that led to."

Angered, Madam Schneider spun on her heel and hissed, "What did you say, you ungrateful barrel of a man?"

Mr. Weber yelled, "The castle has been emptied of every last appointee! What else did you expect to hear?"

Mr. Meyer followed, "How will the court continue to function like this? Who will handle the judicial system, taxation, and diplomatic affairs?"

"My men are *camping* outside the walls," Mr. Lang added. "Security is in disarray. They have no towers, no weapons, no plan, not even enough cloth to make tents to sleep in."

She charged towards them; the men retreated cautiously. Mr. Weber reminded her, "Ten paces, Madam Schneider, ten paces!"

Madam Schneider glared at them. "You ungrateful lot. Had I not gone down on my knees swearing to Lady Alicia you could be trusted, you wouldn't have been between these walls right now. You wouldn't even be between the walls of your own homes!"

"What?"

"You think this is bad?" Madam Schneider hissed. "She *ordered* every man imprisoned."

"You're joking. Every man in this castle? Do you have any idea how many men work—"

"No, Mr. Weber," she interrupted, "not just in this castle. In *town*."

The awkward silence was disrupted by the sudden blast of a pistol. It sent wild screams into the air as everyone scrambled to the walls or ducked for cover.

They looked back at the gathered maids behind them and realized that one of them had accidentally pulled the trigger as she and one of her friends were examining the pistol.

Madam Schneider yelled, "WHO FIRED THAT SHOT?"

Face down and holding the pistol in her palms, a maid said under her breath, "She was just showing me how it works."

The other maid took the pistol from her friend's hand. "Give me that! I didn't tell you to pull the trigger."

"You said *pull.*"

"I said: *and thennn, you pull.* As in: you pull to shoot, *later.* But you don't pull while it was still pointed at my face!"

Pale-faced, the men turned their gazes to Madam Schneider.

She cleared her throat. "Erza... A knife will suit you better."

"Yes, Madam Schneider. I'm sorry."

Summoning a smile, Madam Schneider assured the men, "There. Everything is under control. Now, as I was saying: the shocking revelation of the details of how *human romance* is performed was a little too much, too sudden, for Lady Alicia's pure heart, as it would have been for any damsel of her age. I ask you to understand that Alicia has been sheltered from the world her whole life. She was not prepared for this. It will take a few days for the shock to pass."

"A few DAYS?"

"In the meantime, my efforts have spared the whole town the toll of Lady Alicia's panic and allowed *you* to maintain a foothold in this castle. Be grateful for what you've got. Work with it. And let us hold on until our lady overcomes this *temporary stage* or until the return of our lord."

At the tip of her words, another shot was fired from the opposite structure, maids' screams burst into the air, and a bullet shattered the window above the men's heads.

From the opposite building, a maid with a musket threw her upper half through the window to yell, "Did anyone get hurt? You, in the main building's third floor, did that shot kill anyone?"

Not flinching, not moving a muscle, Madam Schneider continued addressing the men as if nothing had happened. "Yes, let us hold on. I'm sure God will not abandon us."

Chapter 9

Alicia & Priest

Mr. Weber sighed as he sat on the small wooden chair in the dark and quiet atmosphere of the tight place, shrouded by the calming scent of matured wood and incense.

He sighed some more, joined his hands together and lowered his head, then said calmly, "Forgive me father, for I have sinned."

A wooden slide slowly crept open, and a man said with a soothing voice, "God—the father of all mercies—through the death and resurrection of his only Son has reconciled the world to himself and sent the Holy Spirit among us for the forgiveness of sins… Strengthen your heart, my son. Embrace the faith. Tell me, what is the sin you seek forgiveness for?"

"Father, I am not sure I should be saying this in God's house, but recently, I feel lost. I feel like a lost lamb. Powerless. A numskull. Yet this lamb is expected to keep the gates of hell from blasting wide open and burning the world. And I have no idea how to keep that from happening but through the ministry of the Church and its holy priests to give me guidance. You see: Princess Alicia—"

The slide quickly shut.

"Hey!" Mr. Weber raged as he struggled to open the slide against the priest in the other section. "I said I need God's help!"

"You have no help here, Weber. Go somewhere else!"

"What kind of a priest are you, turning down a lost lamb before he even starts?"

"A sane one!"

Mr. Weber groaned aloud and pulled harder, causing the slide to break.

"Father Gianni…? Father Gianni, I know you're in there."

Father Gianni's skinny, well-shaved, scrawny face with deep wrinkles and tonsured head peeked through the broken slide hole and barked, "WHAT?"

Mr. Weber sighed. "Look, Father, I need your help with Alicia."

"Oh, you want *my help*, again? Wasn't last time humiliating enough?"

Mr. Weber tried to calm Gianni down. "*Come onnn,*

you're still upset about that? So, she made a teeny, tiny, little joke about your hair, big deal."

Father Gianni yelled, "She called my head *brighter than my future*!"

"That was just an innocent—"

"And she asked her maids if the reflection of my *shiny bald pate* is how God knows where all his priests are!"

Mr. Weber froze for a moment, then asked, "Does he?"

Father Gianni stuck his head through the tight hole, touching his hair. "This is my Tonsure, a symbol of my humility and devotion to God. It is every priest's loftiness and joy. And Spoiled Alicia MADE FUN OF IT!"

"Hey, hey, hey!" Mr. Weber raised his voice in panic. He then opened the door to peek outside the confession chamber before retreating back inside.

Mr. Weber warned, "I did not hear that, understand? Do not call her *spoiled*, or we won't have to worry how much hair on our heads we still got left because we won't have any heads on our shoulders at all."

"Still got left? It didn't fall off! I shave it!"

"Yes, yes, yes, that's not the point. The point is, you are a priest of God—the father of all mercies—how can you still be upset about something that happened two years ago? She was only ten years old. A child."

"That *child* brought down the church I helped her father build for her. And no one would even to tell me why, up 'till now."

Cornered, Mr. Weber made up a quick excuse. "It's—the structure wasn't sound. It was, um, tilted. Yes, that was it, if I recall correctly. A simple matter of safety, nothing more."

"It was built on *stone*."

"Let us not argue with architects. Now, I know you better than to believe you could possibly hold a grudge over things so small. Over anything, as a matter of fact. You are a priest, for God's sake! And now is the time of God's calling for you. Father Gianni. We need you. I need you. And Princess Alicia needs you."

"What does Spoiled Al—*Agghh!*"

Father Gianni screamed in pain, and his head retreated to his side of the chamber as Mr. Weber suddenly, accidentally, poked his eye when he tried to silence him.

"Son of a—*Agghh!* That hurt!"

Mr. Weber said, restless with guilt, "Father Gianni, no cursing in the house of God, please."

"You poked my eye!"

"I was aiming for your mouth… Father Gianni?"

"What?"

"About Spoiled Alicia—"

"You just called her Spoiled."

"I certainly did not..." Mr. Weber straightened on his seat, eyes darting left and right. "Will you please look at me when I'm talking to you?"

Father Gianni's head reached through the hole again, eye blinking rapidly.

"We need your help," Mr. Weber resumed. "It looks like Princess Alicia has reached that *certain age* of her life and has found out about *the thing*."

"What thing?"

"*The thing*. You know, the thing, how, um—" Mr. Weber explained with hand signals.

"Ah! *That* thing?"

"Yes, and it caused her slight distress. She is not coping with it too well, I'm afraid. So, we thought—in the absence of her father—who is better suited to fulfill the role of explaining these things to her than you?"

Father Gianni raised an eyebrow. "What about Madam Schneider? What about her comfort-maids and guidance-maids? Why don't they explain it to her?"

"They tried, Father Gianni, they tried. But it's just not

the same as it would have been coming from a trusted, assuring, fatherly figure such as our lord or *yourself, of course*."

"Ah!"

"She needs to learn from your experience—"

Father Gianni yelped, "My experience? Mr. Weber, I'm a priest."

"*I meant,* she needs someone she relies on to assure her pure, innocent, Christian heart that this is not necessarily an *evil thing*. Wash all those unnecessary worries *awayyy*. Father Gianni, you understand what I'm asking of you?"

"Hmm."

"On the other hand, not that I'm suggesting you're interested in such things, Father Gianni, but just imagine how grateful our lord would be to have such a sensitive, uncomfortable task taken off his shoulders. As a father myself, I can tell you for certain I'd be most appreciative to have someone trustworthy explain these matters to my own daughter better than I could ever do. Oh, what a relief that would be, what peace of mind! It would only be appropriate to award a *suitable donation* worthy of such effort."

Father Gianni stared at him for a moment. "I'll see what I can do."

"Excellent," replied Mr. Weber. "We must be on our way then, quickly, while Madam Schneider can still secure us a temporary permit into the castle. My coach is waiting for us outside."

"Permit? Wait… Mr. Weber, what permit?"

* * *

In the dark dungeons beneath the castle, Mr. Weber slowly dragged an old chair over the uneven stone floor. He set it in front of a cell and sat on it with a great sigh.

Father Gianni lay behind bars. He was all beaten up, black-eyed, scratches of fingernails across his face, his robes torn, roughed pages sticking out of the edges his bible, and a bullet wound to his foot.

"I left you with her for only *one minute*…" said Mr. Weber. "Mind telling me what happened?"

Father Gianni muttered, his eyes disoriented, "And the Lord said: I am the light of the world. Whoever follows me will never walk in darkness, but will have the light of life— Oh Lord, so true are your words. I've seen the light. I've seen the light. The *liiight*." He wept with joy, hands clutched tightly to the bible at his chest.

Mr. Weber snapped his fingers repeatedly. "Hey! Father Gianni, snap out of it. I'm trying to get you out of this mess."

Father Gianni jolted. "What, what, who...? Oh, Mr. Weber, when did you get here?"

"What, you didn't see me drag this chair? Now, work with me here. I'm trying to help. I asked you: what in the world happened between Princess Alicia and you after I left the two of you together?"

"Nothing. There was, uh... I'm not sure I remember."

"I heard Alicia scream."

"Oh, yes, yes. There was a scream, and then, and then, suddenly, there was... *A divine happening.*"

"Divine happening?"

"And I had an epiphany."

"An epiphany?"

"Yes. A miracle, Mr. Weber, *a miracle*. I saw a swirl of colors flash before my eyes. A beautiful, swirling, dazzling colors of white, and red, and pink, and blue, and brown, and green, and yellow."

"What, Father Gianni, what are you talking about? What colors?"

"I've never seen so many women's legs in my life, Mr. Weber. *Sooo many, beautiful, slender, smooth legs...* And they were all kicking."

Eyes wide, Mr. Weber muttered in disbelief, "You were peeking at the maids' underwear while you were getting your ass kicked?"

"Underwear. Yes. That's what it was. But not all."

"Not—Father Gianni!" Mr. Weber raged in disbelief.

"And then, I heard a woman's voice, calling in the wilderness: *Call the nurses! Call the nurses!* Call the nurses for whom, or for what? I did not know. I just lay there, and I was *sooo happy—aw, aw, aww!*" He yelped with pain as Mr. Weber reached out and pulled Father Gianni's hair.

Mr. Weber yelled, "Will you snap out of it already, you perverted excuse of a priest! You creep!" He let go. "Snap out of it. Go back a little and tell me what made Alicia scream like that in the first place? Why did her maids beat you?"

"Oh, yes. I remember now. I was, I was trying to explain to her the spiritual aspect behind human love. And when I said the words *'all men,'* I think that's when it dawned on her."

"What dawned on her?"

"That I'm a man, too."

"And you were—"

"Less than ten paces away. Yes. Much less. The maids had thought Spoiled Alicia allowed it because I'm a priest. They didn't realize that, until that moment, she had not seen me as anything but these robes I wear. So, when I said the words *'all men,'* she frowned at me, and she screamed *'HE*

Spoiled Alicia

HAS ONE, TOO!' and the beating started."

"Ah!"

Chapter 10

Alicia & Permanent Solution

Frowning, Alicia was so mad, she *personally* flipped through the pages of the book at her desk while her reading-maids ran all over the castle's library, searching for books.

"And he dares call himself a *Man of God*. What kind of a Godly man will allow himself to walk around with a malicious thing like that hidden under his robes!"

Alicia slapped the book off her desk. "This is useless!" She turned to her busy maids. "Have you found one yet?"

"We're searching, my lady."

"Keep looking. There must be an answer to this-this catastrophe in one of these books. A way to eradicate that evil from this world. Keep looking!"

Suddenly, Alicia snapped with shock as her eyes caught sight of something she had not seen before.

She walked to the center of the two spiral staircases leading to the upper floors of the castle's library and gazed up to the second floor where one of her reading-maids stood atop a sliding-ladder, searching, picking out and putting back books into one of the high shelves.

Alicia stared up at the maid for a little pause with eyes full of curiosity.

"You there," Alicia ordered, "come down here."

The reading-maid hurried down the ladder and the stairs. She approached Alicia. "Yes, my lady?"

"What's that thing under your skirt?"

Shocked, the poor maid's cheeks reddened. She stammered, "What? Nothing, nothing."

"That was not nothing. I saw it. What are you hiding down there?"

The other maids passing close by, books at hand, stopped in their tracks when they heard this. Their gazes became fixed upon their friend.

One maid asked, shocked, "Elyse, you stole something?"

"What, nooo! Of course not!" the maid, Elyse, yelped. "My lady, I swear to you, I would never—"

Alicia interrupted, "I didn't say you stole anything. I asked what are you hiding down there."

"Nothing, I'm not hiding anything."

"Show it to me."

"My lady, it's just a… My God, how do I say this?"

Alicia grimaced. "I said, show it to me, *now*."

Dismayed, Elyse nervously spun on her toes left and right as she turned her face among her fellow maids, who pierced her with their eyes.

"Yes, but, one moment, just…" She leaned towards Alicia to whisper, "Can we please not do this here?" She signaled towards the other maids with her eyes. "*Please*?"

Alicia raised an eyebrow. She ordered, "Everyone, leave us alone."

Elyse sighed in relief as her friends left and shut the doors behind them.

"Well? Come one," Alicia said.

"Do we really have to? I mean…" she stammered with an uneasy smile, but before her mistress's fiery gaze, Elyse surrendered.

Her cheeks apple-red, Elyse looked away and raised her skirt up to her waist.

Alicia bent down, her eyes nailed to the strange thing Elyse wore. "What is this?"

"It's a chastity belt."

"Chastity belt?"

Elyse explained, embarrassed, "It's-it's not what you

think. It's not that I'm a bad girl or anything, I swear, it's just that, my father, well, he, he's just that kind of a person, a little bit of a scaredy-cat and, and, my lady, can you please not stare so close? It's making me nervous."

Alicia kept staring. "What is it for?"

"*It'sss,* what else? It's to protect me from, from, unwanted, *you know*. Oh God, we really should not be talking about such improper things."

Alicia poked the big lock with her finger. "Can it be removed?"

"Only with the key or, I don't know, maybe a big hammer?"

Alicia straightened up at last. The maid dropped her skirt with a great sigh.

"So, if this is what I think it's for: while you're wearing it, men cannot…"

"Yes. It's impossible."

Alicia glared into Elyse's eyes for a short pause, then suddenly poked Elyse's forehead. "Why didn't you say something? You've seen me searching all this time."

"I'm sorry, I didn't really know what we were looking for."

Alicia had already barged towards the door. Elyse raced her to it and opened the door for her mistress. The rest of the maids waited outside.

She ordered, "Get me a hammer and *the toughest maid I've got.*"

* * *

Madam Schneider and Mr. Meyer, followed by a couple of armed maids, were on their way to see Father Gianni when they saw Mr. Weber exit the door that led to the dungeons.

"We've heard about what happened to Father Gianni," said Madam Schneider. "How is he?"

"Good, good! Yes, he's doing great. He, um, he's not taking any visitors right now." Mr. Weber closed the door behind him. "He's doing some bible reading, I believe."

"Bible reading?" asked Mr. Meyer.

"Yes. He has much to reflect on, and he doesn't wish to be disturbed. You know, embracing the opportunity of, um, the quiet atmosphere, and all."

"I see."

Madam Schneider said, "Well, so long as he's doing fine. Mr. Weber, I'm glad to have found you here, as I should probably tell you that less than an hour ago, Lady Alicia sent a letter about the *small crisis* she believes we have, asking for help."

"Oh God, no. She wrote to her father?"

"No. The pope."

Mr. Weber's eyes looked as though they were about to pop out of his head. "KILL ALL MESSENGERS!" he screamed.

"Mr. Weber—"

"THE HORSES, SHOOT THEM IN THE LEGS, CLOSE ALL THE GATES, DO SOMETHING! STOP THAT LETTER!"

"MR. WEBER!" Mr. Meyer raised his voice. "Are you implying that you want us to intercept a letter sent by our own monarch? Sabotaging her communication lines?"

"Yes! Yes! I am implying."

"*Outrageous comportment.* Such betrayal of a confidant that borders the limit of treason is not just beyond consideration, it is unbefitting of a castle's hirelings, much less its councilors. Mr. Weber, I am both shocked and sickened to my core by your words." he hissed, before he produced a letter from his sleeve. "I did, however, find this letter lying on the floor, somewhere."

"Oh!" Mr. Weber snatched the letter from Mr. Meyer and read it.

"Also—and this is only a rumor—I heard that a certain

messenger has suddenly decided to take his family and leave to Venice."

"Yes, smart lad, the weather there is splendid this time of year," said Mr. Weber, still reading the letter.

"What does it say?" asked Madam Schneider.

"Well, to put it mildly, if I didn't already know what's going on, I'd leave the Holy See immediately and come running to see what in the world is this *'devil's plot in process that threatens the very fabric of our Christian world'* is all about," Mr. Weber said before he hid the letter his clothes. "It doesn't seem that urgent."

He then turned to the other two and hissed, "This has gone far enough. We must put an end to this before it snowballs out of control."

* * *

Mr. Schmidt—the town's blacksmith—was a short, bellied man with a bald head, wide nose, thick white beard, and great muscular arms.

He was summoned before Alicia in a hurry. He was still wearing his shop's leather apron as he entered the castle's library and stood across a small table from Alicia.

Spoiled Alicia

Mr. Schmidt lowered his hat. "I came as soon as I heard, Princess. How may I be of service? What's the emergency?"

Alicia's maids were suddenly on alert when Mr. Schmidt took a step forward.

Clueless, he froze in place and looked between the frowning maids, whom Alicia signaled to stand down.

"Mr. Schmidt," Alicia called, "you're the one who made the castle guards' armor, is that correct?"

"Some of them, yes. Others were made by colleagues from surrounding towns or might have been in use since the time of my grandfather, even. You see, my lady, our family has been in business for a long time."

"And have you made any craftier items before? Something with a lot more details and precision."

"I made a few things in my time, yes."

Alicia motioned to a maid with her head and said to Mr. Schmidt, "This is what we're dealing with."

The maid set a plate on the table with a cucumber in the middle and two tomatoes to one end.

Mr. Schmidt looked strangely at the plate. His face, and Alicia's, slowly followed one tomato as it rolled towards the other end.

The maid put the tomato back in place.

Now the second tomato rolled!

A second maid grabbed the first tomato, intending to bring it to the other end, just as the first maid had grabbed the second tomato, intending to put it back.

The two maids argued with their hands for a moment—wrists and fingers interlocked—which tomato should go where. The first maid flipped the cucumber the other way, causing the second maid to yell with frustration, "IT DOESN'T MATTER WHICH END!"

Embarrassed, the two maids then stood at attention, hands joined in front of them. A tomato still rolled halfway across plate. Again, one of the maids swiftly put it back and assumed her previous pose.

Alicia cleared her throat. "So, as I was saying, *this* is what we are dealing with."

Uncertain, Mr. Schmidt asked, "Vegetables?"

A maid approached Mr. Schmidt and whispered what the vegetables were supposed to represent.

Mr. Schmidt turned his face towards her, speechless, his eyes wide.

"Elyse," Alicia called with a signal of her hand.

Elyse peeked left and right at her friends. Her cheeks reddened with embarrassment as she approached with a cloth at hand and set it on the table. The item wrapped with the cloth made a loud clang against the wood. Elyse inhaled a deep breath, shut her eyes, and unveiled the chastity belt and broken lock concealed in the cloth.

She returned to her spot with her palms tucked into the folds of her skirt, between her thighs, not daring to raise her face lest she saw the looks her friends were giving her.

"*This* is the answer to that problem," Alicia declared firmly. "And you are going to make it for me."

Embarrassed, Mr. Schmidt double-checked, "You, um, forgive me for asking this, but just to be clear: you want me to make your ladyship a, uhm, a belt like it?"

"Don't be ridiculous. Of course not!"

"I…don't…really…understand."

"It's simple." Alicia glared daggers at him. "Why should I be the one to wear this thing when it is *your gender* who caused the problem in the first place?"

"Problem?" Mr. Schmidt asked. He was yet still clueless to what was going on. His gaze fixed on the maids lined behind Alicia, who nodded their heads with approval of their mistress.

"You are going to combine these two items together and make a chastity belt for *mennn*."

"Ah!" was all that Mr. Schmidt had to respond with.

"How fast can you make it?" asked Alicia.

"Well, um, it's not that complicated. I mean, it's only a shell, and I already have all the right parts. So, um, I think if I work on it for the rest of the day, then I can have it ready by tomorrow morning."

"Excellent."

An old man's perverted and awfully creepy look flashed through Mr. Schmidt's eyes. He snatched the chastity belt. "I might have to take the belt with me for, um, for reference, of course."

Elyse buried her face in her palms.

"Done."

* * *

When Mr. Meyer, Mr. Weber, and Madam Schneider arrived at the castle's library, determined to confront Alicia, they found Charlotte standing at the door, hammer in hand.

"Is Princess Alicia inside?" asked Mr. Meyer.

"Her ladyship is busy with a meeting and does not wish to be disturbed."

"A meeting? With whom?"

The door opened from the other end, prompting Charlotte to move out of the way, and a very delighted Mr.

Spoiled Alicia

Schmidt walked out, a warm chastity belt in his palms.

The three trailed Mr. Schmidt with their eyes before Alicia came out of the room, too.

"Princess Alicia," Mr. Meyer started.

"We need to talk," Madam Schneider followed.

Mr. Weber added, "Excluding all men from the castle's grounds has created an unusual environment. We are unable to get any work done, a middle ground must be established."

Alicia signaled them to be silent. "Relax, Mr. Weber, and all of you... Yes, I am well aware, as Madam Schneider has not stopped reminding me about this all day."

Mr. Weber said, "Then my lady does acknowledge the severity of the situation."

"Of course," Alicia assured him. "Trust that I have not been standing idle about this, and a solution has been found."

The three adults froze in place for a moment.

"It has?" asked Mr. Meyer.

"Yes. Starting tomorrow morning, the guards and officials of the court will be allowed to return to the castle."

Mr. Weber clapped his hands together. "Well, um, that's good, that's good." He looked at the other two. "I guess we were worried over nothing, then." He turned back to Alicia. "Well, um, now that there's no issue left to talk about whatsoever, we must thank you for your tolerance and noble, truly noble and selfless understanding. And do please forgive us had we shown any overreaction to the matter, at any point."

"Your worries are understandable," Alicia assured him. She added just before she left, "As such, you are all invited to my rose gardens tomorrow morning for the new product's demonstration."

The three of them stared, clueless, at Alicia's back as she headed down the hallway.

"What product?"

Chapter 11

Alicia & The Blacksmith Who Saved The Day

"Goodness!" was Madam Schneider's only reaction.

She stood in the rose gardens with Mr. Weber, Mr. Meyer, Mr. Lang, and a flock of Alicia's maids.

With widened eyes and bodies stiffer than the logs of trees, not a single person in the garden was able to peel their eyes off the belt with its shiny, polished metal piece molded to the shape of a man's member: livid, fully erect, mighty and twisted, with puffed veins and large balls made with remarkable detail. Placed over a velvet cushion, the belt glistened with vicious spark under the morning's sun.

"It looks angry," commented Mr. Meyer.

Mr. Weber turned to Mr. Schmidt, "You know, Mr. Schmidt, I've been to your shop once before, and I've seen the things you sell in there. They're *all*, well, how do I say this? Pretty conventional. But well-made and fairly priced."

"Thank you."

"My point is: in all the *years and yeeears* you've been in business, YOU DECIDED TO GET ARTISTIC NOW?"

Mr. Schmidt asked, clueless, "What's wrong with it?"

"Everything is wrong with it!"

"I don't understand."

Mr. Lang joined the conversation, "I believe what Mr. Weber is trying to say is, did you had to make it with so much detail?"

"It really looks angry," said Mr. Meyer, unable to take his eyes off the item.

Nervous, Mr. Schmidt waved his arms. "I, I thought this is what you wanted, you know, nothing short from the best my hands can create. I did mold it after the only one I know."

Hearing this, Madam Schneider and all the maids now secretly stole inquisitive looks at Mr. Schmidt, totally impressed. The men lost their voices for a moment.

Mr. Weber stammered, "Well, uh, the source doesn't really matter, it's all the same, or so I've been told."

Mr. Meyer pulled Mr. Weber's sleeve and whispered, his eyes glued to the item and his voice maimed with despair, "This mustn't be allowed."

"I know, I know."

"It really mustn't be allowed."

"I said I know."

"Can you imagine the face of our lord when the guards line up for his return with that thing strapped to them?" asked a pale-faced Mr. Lang.

Madam Schneider whispered, "We have to talk Alicia out of this. We'll be the laughingstock of the whole world for a thousand years if we don't stop it."

"I said I know, all right. I'm thinking," Mr. Weber said.

"Perhaps if we…add some color…camouflage the tip somehow? It might become…less intimidating," Mr. Lang muttered.

Just then, Alicia arrived in the rose gardens. She threw a disgusted, yet curious look at the item Mr. Schmidt created and asked, "Is this it?"

"Yes, my lady."

She turned to her counselors and smiled. "Well, what do you think?"

Silence…

"We are not really sure," Mr. Weber said at last.

"You don't like it?"

Mr. Meyer poked Mr. Weber's side. Mr. Weber pleaded, "Lady *Aliciaaa, please*, is there really a need for any of this? I mean, *come onnn*, the councilors and the guards have been serving the castle for years and years."

She frowned. "Mr. Weber, let me make it clear: I don't know how other women were able to tolerate this *malice* running around, unchecked, for so long, but unless evil is restrained for certain, then for the sake of myself and all women, I cannot restore my faith in any of you. Especially when I've been assured by more than a single source that, sometimes," she glared at them with narrowed gaze, "it cannot be *controlled*. Isn't that correct?"

"Well, um, you see—"

"Lady *Aliciaaa*—"

"The chastity belt, or work from beyond the walls. These are my conditions."

Building on what he had heard, Mr. Schmidt was able to form an idea about what was going on around him. He stepped forward and asked, "Princess Alicia, if I may."

"Yes, Mr. Schmidt?"

"It seems to me that my lady wishes for me to reproduce quite a number of the belt you've ordered. If that is the case, then I'm afraid that I must have misunderstood your intention earlier, and the model I've made is not practical."

Alicia frowned. "Why is that?"

"Well, for one thing, creating a belt like this requires

much work, time, and expense. I mean, just imagine how much time it's going to take me to measure and make one for every individual. I could make a belt or two a day, at best. That's not going to work. However, if I may offer an alternative…"

Mr. Schmidt took an orange from a plate of fruits set on a table, ripped half the shell clean from the orange with his bare hand and covered the model he had created with it.

Everyone breathed with relief as they could finally look elsewhere.

Alicia watched what Mr. Schmidt did with much doubt, "How is that going to work? How can a stick like that be contained within a sphere that's not even half its extension?"

"It will work, my lady, I assure you. You have my word."

"You're absolutely sure?"

"Of course. Not only will it work perfectly as you intend it to, but also, now that it's so simple, my workers and I can make dozens a day. It will save so much time, and if I may add: it will be economically sound."

Alicia mulled over it for a moment, tapping her hand fan to her chin. "But unlike the first model, how will I know that it's properly equipped, rather than left at ones' home…? Can you make it so that it is worn over their clothes and clearly visible?"

"Leave the details to me."

Alicia turned to her councilors. "What do you think?"

Madam Schneider poked Mr. Weber's side, whispering, "Take the deal. Take it."

"Take the deal," Mr. Meyer whispered.

Mr. Lang whispered, "Take it, take it! I might be able to pass it as part of the guards' new armor and no one will notice, take it."

Mr. Meyer added, "We can wear very wide belts, it won't be visible."

"You've seen the alternative. Don't be stupid. Taaake it." Said Mr. Lang.

Mr. Weber cleared his voice and stepped forward. "If it pleases our lady, the council *approves* the use of the new belt."

Alicia turned to Mr. Schmidt. "Excellent work. Begin production immediately."

"As you wish."

Alicia left, throwing over her shoulder, "Once all councilors and castle guards are chastened properly, you can start with town's people. I'll personally mandate it."

Everybody stiffened, and their eyes widened. They couldn't believe their ears. "The town's people, too?"

Spoiled Alicia

* * *

The four guards were messing around with their new chastity belts, which they yet thought was a joke, and had discovered a new game.

They were competing to see who would break the longest distance.

Three of the guards held their fourth friend in the air by his arms and legs, face-down, and swung him back and forth as they counted, "One... Two... *Threeee.*"

They threw him onto the polished marble floor of the long hallway, where he landed on the metal sphere of his chastity belt, rubbed with butter, and slid to the end of the hallway—his body arched and his limbs raised off the floor—his friends' laughter at his back.

Passing his friends' previous record, he cheered a wild, "*Yesss! Woohoo!*"

His friends were silent. Confused, he looked over his shoulder from where he lay on the floor and saw his friends standing at attention in their spots. Turning his face the other way, he saw a woman's dress.

Alicia and her maids stood right in front of him.

Overtaken by surprise, the guard jumped to his feet at

full attention, backed towards the wall, and shouted, "Yes. The belt has passed the test, and it's holding firm, sir!"

The women clearly didn't buy it. They moved on, shaking their heads.

"It doesn't get stupider than that," a maid whispered to her friend.

One of Alicia's maids thought she had heard a noise and lagged behind the rest as she looked through a window.

Her eyes widened with embarrassment.

Atop the tower across from the building she was in, there were two guards behaving with absolute foolishness:

They were dancing around like monkeys! Each held two stick in their hands, throwing them in the air like true performers, and banged them against the metal sphere of their belts like drums—making music.

* * *

Naturally, Alicia didn't allow the guards to keep the keys to their own chastity belts. She assigned a maid to keep the keys for every guard or two.

Maids and guards stood in waiting or seated themselves in long lines that extended far outside the makeshift workshop where Mr. Schmidt and his craftsmen were creating the belts.

Mr. Schmidt was busily hammering another metal piece when a guard cut the line.

"*Heeyyy*, Mr. Schmidt. I could use a little help here," the guard yelled cheerfully.

Mr. Schmidt raised his face and saw the guard, Adalwolf, approaching him with a wide smile whilst playing his unlocked chastity belt in the air.

"What happened? How did you unlock the belt?"

Adalwolf was a very big man with a black beard and outstanding height. He had a very relaxed and humorous personality and was a well-known womanizer.

He leaned over Mr. Schmidt's table, smiling. "Listen, uh, we've got a small problem."

"Something wrong with the belt?"

"No, no, the belt works fine. It's just that," he leaned even closer to whisper, "it's a little bit tight around the, *you know*."

"Ah! The metal piece?"

"Yes, I was wondering if you could perhaps make it just a little bit bigger."

Mr. Schmidt examined the belt in his hands. He raised an eyebrow. "How much bigger?"

"Like, about, you know, maybe this much."

All the guards and maids in line were leaning to the sides now, curiously following the hushed conversation and Adalwolf's hand signals... Their eyes suddenly widened.

Mr. Schmidt blinked in surprised. "Ohh! That much?" He examined the belt again, then said, "I'll see what I can do. Come back in an hour."

"Thanks, you're the best." Adalwolf slapped Mr. Schmidt on the shoulder and went on his way.

The maids followed him with eyes glittering in admiration, whereas the waiting guards shook their heads in astonishment. Once Adalwolf exited the workshop, the guards' faces turned in unison towards Mr. Schmidt.

Chapter 12

Alicia & New Design

Sitting at her dining table early in the morning, Alicia had interrupted the breakfast process, set her cheek on the palm of her hand, and glared with suspicious eyes at the guards standing on either end of the hall.

Feeling their mistress's gaze upon them, the guards stiffened, secretly peeking looks back at her with the corner of their eyes.

Alicia crocked her finger to one of her breakfast-maids, who bent lower, and asked quietly. "Is it just me, or do their belts look bigger than yesterday's?"

The maid whispered back, "I'm sure it's just a trick of the light, my lady."

Alicia hummed and signaled the breakfast-maid off with her hand.

Just then, Mr. Weber entered the dining hall, stealing the spotlight as he strolled like a peacock, with a wide smile on his face.

The maids' glares followed him, their eyebrows raised

with shock, while the rest of the councilors looked like their eyes were about to pop out of their heads when they saw him walk in.

Mr. Weber had not opted for the larger version, like everyone else. In fact, his belt looked even smaller than the size Mr. Schmidt first made.

Instead, Mr. Weber's chastity belt's piece was made of polished, glittering gold engraved with royal patterns.

He stood next to the other councilors, who couldn't help but lean forward a little to curiously peek at his piece.

Mr. Weber peeked back at theirs and said quietly with a smug smirk, "Hah! It is not the size that matters, *fools*."

"*Outrageous*," Mr. Meyer whispered.

"Tell that to the twenty-something maids who stopped me on my way here."

Mr. Lang cleared his throat and stepped forward. "Lady Alicia, there's a small issue that we need to address. It's a little bit urgent."

"What?"

"The belts, they're not working."

Alicia frowned. "Why?"

"Well, you see, the thing is, my men eventually will need to go."

"Go where?"

"No, not *go* as in *go somewhere*, but just, *go*. Take care of business."

Alicia raised an eyebrow. "And what business would that be?"

Nervous, Mr. Lang spun towards the rest and back to Alicia again. He let it out, "Well, if you don't mind me putting it bluntly: they need to pee."

"Well then, have them do their thing like they always do. What's the problem?"

"The problem is that the maids hold all the keys. Some men were not able to find the maids holding their keys in time. We had…a few incidents yesterday."

Mr. Weber shut his eyes with dismay.

"Is this some kind of an excuse to put men in control of their own keys?"

"Nooo."

"Well then, what is it that you're trying to establish?" asked Alicia. "What does one thing got to do with the other?"

Realizing that Alicia didn't know, Mr. Lang was stunned motionless. He looked among Alicia's maids, pleading, "A little help here… Somebody… *Please?*"

A breakfast-maid looked at Madam Schneider, who nodded with approval. The maid then leaned at Alicia's side.

"My lady, the thing is…" she whispered, before she continued with her explanation in a more hushed tone.

Alicia listened carefully, "Dual-use? What dual-use…? They also use it for what…?"

Alicia fell speechless, and the color slowly drained from her face.

She stood up and ran out of the dining hall, shutting the door behind her, and let out one horrified scream after another.

Madam Schneider closed her eyes. She said to Mr. Lang, "You might want to tell your men to hold it. This will take some time."

* * *

Following their previous failure to tend after their mistress when needed, Alicia's comfort-maids were reformed—replaced by a new, more efficient set of maids and subjected to stricter rules.

Alicia lay on her back on the white-and-gold couch. Her head rested on the thighs of a comfort-maid who brushed Alicia's hair, while a second maid sat at the opposite end, massaging Alicia's feet and rubbing them with oils.

Spoiled Alicia

A third maid knelt by the couch, painting Alicia's nails.

A fourth maid fanned Alicia's face.

A fifth maid kneeled with a spoon and a cup of citrus juice at hand. Two more maids stood on the other end, their only job to listen to their mistress and approve whatever she said because… Emotions!

Alicia cried her heart out, tears running down her cheeks. "I don't understand it."

Her maids affirmed, "No one does."

"I certainly don't understand it, either."

"*There, thereee.*" A maid wiped Alicia's tears for her.

Alicia said again, "What kind of a world is this where people kill chicken, eat eggs, and poke women with pee-sticks? JUST WHAT IS WRONG WITH THIS CREATION? IT IS HORRIBLE!"

"Horrible, indeed."

"Yes, truly horrible."

"It's all God's fault," said Alicia.

"Absolutely-a…" The maids froze and looked at one another.

"It's all made wrong. Doesn't he realize it? Can't he see how much we're suffering… uh, unm, no, too sour," she said to the maid who watered her lips with juice. "Sweeten it a little."

"Yes."

"And make it chillier."

"Yes, I'm sorry."

Alicia resumed, "Wait until the pope gets here. I'm going to have a serious word with him about this, and if he isn't going to do something about it, then I will."

"You, um, you sure will."

"You be you, my lady. Don't let his Ferula intimidate you."

Alicia straightened up suddenly, her eyes wide. "What am I doing? I've got no time for this. You, all of you, dismissed. I'll call for you later."

As her maids curtsied and left, Alicia got to her feet, and her image-maids approached her to fix the details of her dressing and hair properly.

"I can't be lying around like this. I have responsibilities. My people will not wait in suffering for God to fix his mistake. They need me," she said to herself as the maids worked on her.

"How do I look?" Alicia asked when her maids were done.

"Perfect."

"No princess ever looked so wonderful."

Spoiled Alicia

Alicia headed towards the door, her eyes glittering with determination. "I may not be the one who speaks to God, but I am dominar of my people, and I know exactly what my strengths and weaknesses are."

* * *

"I have expected this problem to happen, Princess, and already come up with a solution," said Mr. Schmidt as he spread out his arm, inviting Alicia into his temporary workshop.

She entered. "I am listening."

"The belt was made in a hurry, as you well know. We were too focused on fast production and the belt's basic function. We had to trust all other details to be solved through other arrangements."

"I can't assign a maid to every man in the castle just in case they need to *do their business*."

"Not to worry, my lady. The real problem initiated from a design error. And an error in design can simply be fixed by a new design. Allow me to show you the new model."

He unveiled the new chastity belt to reveal a smaller hatch at the center of the metal sphere that could be popped opened. The hatch was closed over a burlap string, which seemed to be have been forgotten there by mistake.

Alicia and her maids stared at the new design curiously. "I see what you're getting at."

"Yes, it's a very simple solution. The men can just pop the hatch open and close it themselves, whenever needed, thus there will be no need to remove the whole belt."

"And it doesn't need a lock and key to secure it? What about, *you know*, the purpose of the whole thing."

"Not to worry, that would be impossible with just the hatch so, yes, no lock is needed."

Alicia stared at the new model for a little pause. She asked, "Will the new modification not hamper the production speed?"

"With more manpower at my disposal: not at all. What's more, all belts that were already made can be easily modified, and the cost will only be slightly pricier than the first model."

A maid asked curiously, "What's up with that string hanging out of it?"

"*That* is the brilliance behind the new design," Mr. Schmidt said with a smirk. "As you know, men need to, um, you know, reach out and hold to, um, point their—"

Alicia stopped him, "Understood. No need to explain."

"Thank you."

"So, how does the string help?"

"Because the sphere makes it impossible for the use of ones hands and a bigger hatch would ruin the purpose of the belt, the string will be tied to the tip of the man's, um, piece. They can then open the hatch and just pull the string to, um, point it in the right direction."

Alicia raised an eyebrow. "You believe it will work?"

"Would you like a demonstration?" he said and spread out his arm to one of the maids to test the belt.

Alicia nodded her approval. The maid walked to the belt, flipped the hatch open with her finger, grabbed the string, and pulled.

Suddenly, a wooden stick tied to the string popped an inch out of the hatch, causing the maid to flinch and yelp with surprise.

Mr. Schmidt bellowed a great laugh. "IT WORKS!"

Chapter 13

Alicia & New Order

Early in the morning, Diedrich kissed Olga goodbye and made his way to the door. "I'm heading out to work."

"Oh, *honeyyy*," Olga called.

He turned around and, to his dismay, he saw Olga raising her hand to her side, holding his chastity belt by the tips of her fingers.

"Forgot something?" she said with a smile and a devious gaze.

He said, nervous, as Olga approached him and began securing the belt to him, "Hah! You know, I can't really work with that thing on me."

"It's the castle's orders, and we can't afford to be fined."

"It's ridiculous."

"I totally agree."

"Then why do you look so happy about it?"

"I'm not," she lied through her teeth. "It truly pains me

so much to do this. My heart is weeping for you, *my trusted beloved…* There!" she declared as the belt was firmly secured.

Olga stood on her toes to kiss him. "Don't work yourself too hard."

Diedrich reached for the keys, but Olga swiftly threw her arm out of his reach, intoning a playful, "*Uh-uh-uhhh.* Fines, remember? Now, off you go. See you in the evening."

She nudged him towards the door.

Once outside, a friend passing by called, "Good morning, Diedrich."

"Good morning," he said half-heartedly, feeling like a lashed puppy as he turned his gaze from one passerby to the next, all dressed with male chastity belts.

He sighed and went on his way.

* * *

"Where is the key, then?" a maid demanded, her face a frown.

She was in a hallway in the castle, alone with Adalwolf, who had his back to the wall.

"Love, I swear to you, I don't know. I must have dropped it somewhere," Adalwolf assured her with a big smile on his face while massaging her upper arms with his big hands.

"I let you keep it for only a heartbeat, and you lost it?"

"What can I say? These things happen. I'm so sorry."

"We need to find it. Let's go, now. Where did you drop it?"

"Don't worry, don't worry," he said with a soothing tone. "We'll just ask Mr. Schmidt to make a new one. What's the big deal?"

"No."

"No?"

She raged, her eyes watery, "No, what if someone else finds it? You promised I'm the only one who gets to keep your key. You swore it."

Adalwolf embraced her, calming her down. "Darling, darling, *come onnn*, you worry too much. It's just a lost key. Even if someone else finds it, what does that mean, *hm*? You don't trust me?"

She muttered, trembling with emotion, "I, I do, but…"

"How will they even know it's my key? It's not like it has my name on it or anything, right? Right?"

The maid retreated a step, wiped her runny nose, and smiled. "Yes, you're right. I'm sorry."

"*Theeere*, you see? Everything is fine. Let's just go and

make a new one."

"Yes. But still, the mere thought that another woman might have it—"

"Elena, look at me," Adalwolf gently held her chin, turned her face to him, and wiped a tear off her chin, "key or no key, there can never be another woman for me."

At the tip of his words, another maid passed through the hallway.

The couple retreated a step apart, not to expose their relationship.

The new maid strolled slowly past them, deliberately, lewdly shaking her hips, her lips adorned with an openly inviting smile. She spun on her heel just as she passed them and flashed Adalwolf the key she was hiding in the palm of her hand, mouthing, "*The western balcony.*"

Entranced by her magic, Adalwolf forgot all about the woman he was holding in his arms just a moment ago and mouthed back with a wide smile, "*Be right there.*"

Fear-stricken, he turned his face back to Elena as he realized his secret conversation with the other woman could not have possibly slipped unnoticed.

Her eyes wide with humiliation and disbelief and her face red with ange, Elena's chest heaved in and out, and her hand slowly grabbed the string sticking out of his belt.

Adalwolf raised his open palms to his chest. "Now, Elena, calm down, it's not what you think—*GAAHHhhh*!"

Elena yanked the string with all her might, and Adalwolf collapsed in a heap to the floor, crying with pain, both hands at his groin.

"LIAR!" Elena took off running, covering her face and crying her heart out.

* * *

In the small town's church, Father Gianni was doing the usual service, reading aloud from the bible:

"Your statutes are my heritage forever; they are the joy of my heart. My heart is set on keeping your decrees, to the very end—"

The church goers, mostly from the village's elderly, sat quietly at the benches, some were reading, others nodded their heads with joy.

When he reached the section that reads, "You are my hiding place and my shield; I have put my…" Father Gianni suddenly paused.

He raised his face and realized that all attendees were now staring at his chastity belt.

"Keep your eyes on the bible," he warned them.

* * *

Mr. Weber seemed deep in thought as he walked around Mr. Meyer's desk, reading a document in his hand.

"I see."

"It's not a half-bad suggestion," Mr. Meyer said as he busily wrote something on his desk. "The young man believes that engraving the crest of our lord's coat-of-armor on the chastity belts' metal piece will be a good improvement."

"This cannot be decided at the spot. We need to think this through."

"Agreed. He even drew a sketch to show how it will look like. But the main issue is that we need to verify from a general third-person perspective if it's indeed the right place, before we accept or reject the idea."

"True, true. But if approved, the cost of applying such modification—WHAT THE HELL ARE WE DOING?" Mr. Weber snapped, throwing the document in the air.

Mr. Meyer looked at him. "Is something wrong?"

"IS SOMETHING WRONG? IS THIS REALLY OUR NEW NORMAL?"

"I'm not following."

Mr. Weber raged, "We only agreed to wear these-these-stupid things because we had no choice at the time! I honestly thought it would only be a matter of days before Lady Alicia snapped out of her panic and canceled the whole thing, but obviously, I was wrong. Not only has it been a week already, but also, everybody now wears them! The whole town wears them! We're even planning to send the first shipment of a chastity belts to the surrounding villages! This has gone beyond ridiculous. This is madness."

Mr. Meyer set his quill aside and crossed his hands together. He said calmly, "Mr. Weber, we've been through this before. I still hear a lot of complaints and not a hint of a solution."

Mr. Weber raised his arms and slapped them to his sides. "Because... I have none."

Suddenly tired, Mr. Weber slowly made his way to a chair, collapsed in it, joined his hands together, and stared at the floor with gloom on his face. "I had a dream once... I thought, I honestly thought that one day I would be this *great councilor*, that I would, hah! That I would sit at the tables of kings and bishops, negotiate nationwide trades, influence policies, and mediate peace among kingdoms. Now... Now,

Spoiled Alicia

I find myself unable to influence a twelve-year-old... The Lord has shown me humility, Mr. Meyer. He truly has."

"Her heart is in the right place. She's only trying to help her people."

"The people would be fine if she would just STOP TRYING TO HELP THEM!"

"And what do you suggest? Send word to our lord?"

"And tell him what? *Leave the most important meeting of the year at once and please come back, we cannot handle your twelve-year-old daughter*—Don't be ridiculous."

"Then the status quo will remain, unless you have something else to suggest."

His face mad and sweaty, Mr. Weber made up his mind. "Yes. Yes, I have... We need to make a stand. We need to face her and explain to her that this situation is not acceptable. We must solve this problem before the lord returns, or there will be a hell of an explanation to make. *Spoiled Alicia must be stopped*."

* * *

In her rose gardens, accompanied by Mr. Weber and Madam Schneider, Alicia admired a rose and said, "I don't understand what you are getting at, Mr. Weber."

"Then allow me to clarify," said Mr. Weber. "The new men's chastity law cannot stand as it has proven quite unpopular."

"By whom? The devil…?" She threw him with a glance and walked away. "The law stands, Mr. Weber, and chastity belts production must be accelerated. It is the only way to keep the *devil horn* at bay."

He chased after her, pleading, "Lady Alicia, if you'd *please* reconsider."

"No," she said, not stopping.

"I'm sure there must be another way. Think about your father."

"What about my father?"

"How will he feel about all of this? I mean, forget the belts' unpopularity, he will certainly not be pleased by the extra cost. The financial burden on the treasury—"

"Will be eased by the fines collected from uncomplying villains."

"Lady Alicia, I beg you, there is no villainy at play here. This is just the way things are since God created the world."

"Mistakes have been made."

"Then how about, how about a middle ground that satisfies all parties and still keeps the *devil horn* at bay? My recommendation is: we continue to make the belts and offer them to people for free, just like you want, just let us not make it a law, at least. We, we will even pay incites to encourage people to wear them. It's a great compromise."

"What's the difference? It sounds like an unnecessary waste of money to me."

"The difference is that *now* everyone has to wear them. It's *a law*. Even your father."

Alicia froze in her tracks. Her eyes widened with shock as it dawned on her.

"My father...?" she muttered as she spun slowly towards them. "That's right..."

Mr. Weber froze as he realized he just made things worse, and Madam Schneider buried her face in her hands.

Alicia hissed, her eyes burning with rage, "He has one, too, *doesn't he?*"

* * *

At the castle's main court, all Alicia's councilors had been summoned for an important announcement, alongside a great number of the castle's bannermen, maids, guards, and a flock of the town's people.

Surrounded by silence, Alicia entered in her white-and-gold dress and glittering jewelry and said as she slowly headed towards the head of the court.

"I had wondered before, where did it all begin? And why hadn't anyone tried to stop this before me… But now, it has become clear."

She stopped on her way and glared at her councilors and bannermen.

"So, it is *my father* who is the source of this evil…? *Infected by it… Desires it… Controlled by it…* And its protector, at the very least…… But bring my word to my people *not to worry*, as it is not yet too late."

She continued her way and climbed the dais to her father's throne, where Father Gianni was instructed to wait.

Alicia stared at the throne with mad eyes for a little pause, then motioned with her head to Father Gianni, who, confused, figured out that she wanted him to pick the scepter from the throne and give it to her. So, he did.

She took the diamond-inlaid scepter in her hands and turned towards the crowd.

"If we are to reclaim this world from evil, then we can only begin at one place." She motioned to Father Gianni. "Father?"

Nervously, Father Gianni's eyes darted back and forth

between Alicia and the crowd, unsure what to do, before he opened the bible in a hurry at the section Alicia had instructed him earlier to prepare.

He recited aloud, "These are the words of wisdom and truth, as our Lord, thy God, has spoken…"

Everyone took off their hats, bowed their heads, and made the sign of the cross on their chests.

He read, "Even so every good tree bringeth forth good fruit; but a corrupt tree bringeth forth evil fruit. A good tree cannot bring forth evil fruit, neither can a corrupt tree bring forth good fruit. Every tree that bringeth not forth good fruit is hewn down, and cast into the fire… Amen."

"Amen," the crowd echoed.

"Amen," said Alicia.

She raised her face to them. "Thus, as the Lord commands us, let us bring down the corrupt tree with our own hands and plant the good one instead. One that is pure. One that is in the image of God. One that is neither corrupt nor touched by the devil. So that from here on forth, only a good fruit can bringeth to our world and our homes."

There was a murmur among the crowd accompanied by shocked, disbelieving faces.

The maids set their palms on their weapons, anxious with anticipation.

Mr. Weber raised his voice and asked, "You're going to dethrone your own father?"

Smiling, Alicia sat on her father's throne. A maid approached her and raised the crown over Alicia's head, calling aloud, "All hail Alicia, lady of her castle and mistress of the worlds!"

And the maid set the crown on her mistress's head.

Anxious eyes shifted left and right, not knowing what to do…

Her maids were the first to fall to their knees, followed by Madam Schneider, then the guards, then the town's people, until everyone bent at the knee, echoing in unison:

"Hail Alicia, lady of her castle and mistress of the worlds!"

"God help us," Mr. Weber whispered to himself.

The guards atop the castle walls fired twenty shots from the cannons, declaring the event.

"And so," Alicia smiled, "my reign begins."

The End

Thank You!

I hope you enjoyed a good read and that you will choose to share this experience with your friends

& don't miss out on the chance to tell the world what you think, by posting your review on Amazon!

For all enquiries
please contact the author at
James.Starvoice@gmail.com

Printed in Great Britain
by Amazon